CRIME,
PUNISHMENT
AND MARS BARS

KENNETH BRIDGES

To Laura

From

Kenny

1

Not drunk is he who from the floor
Can rise alone and still drink more.
William Makepeace Thackeray

Be sober, be vigilant; because your adversary the devil, as a roaring lion, walketh about, looking for anyone to devour.
Peter 5:8

Powerful, dark ,disturbing and often hilarious, this is the gripping story one man's journey through life. He has a perspective on events that is alien to most, seeking the outrageous revenge of the sociopath for perceived slights, without realising he has crossed the borders of 'acceptable' behaviour. An uneasy read.

With many thanks to Blair for help in the production of this book and Kris for the cover design.

CONTENTS

1   Crime Punishment and Mars Bars

2   Meet the Grandparents

3   A Mafia Wedding

4   Schooldays Were Murder

5   Work – A Creepy Experience

6   Starting Lines, Finishing Lines

7   Another Job, One That Took The Biscuit

8   University-A Spot of Upward Mobility

9   Marriage- Nice Pussy

10 The Hoover Man

11 Mary in the Madhouse

12 The Favour

13 Body Parts in Bangkok

CRIME PUNISHMENT AND MARS BARS

There is inevitably a seminal point in the downfall of an individual. With Dostoevsky's anti-hero it was the murder of the old money-lender and her sister, with Hitler it was the ill-advised invasion of the Soviet-Union, consequently denying him world domination. I could have blamed my fall into the chasm of despair on my grandparents and other insane relations, but the real reason for my life of debauchery and ungodliness was a Mars Bar. This apparently innocuous confectionary was to lead me to an existence of squalor and unbearable guilt and turn me into the monster I am today.

I was fourteen years old, working as a paper-delivery boy with a large chain store in East Kilbride, when things started to go wrong. It was there I discovered how much I enjoyed stealing things and my journey into the valley of sin began, a trip that led to the death of three unfortunate humans and an innocent cat. I still had a slight sense of morality in that I wouldn't steal from friends or beat up old ladies, but R.S. McColl was an entirely different story. I didn't have a clue who he was (I imagined him as an Ebenezer Scrooge like character, sitting in his attic counting out all the money he'd made from me staggering about at seven on frosty mornings delivering all his fucking papers, my hands blue with the cold of a Scottish winter.) My father and my uncle, being lefties, had installed in me a strong belief in redistributing the wealth of society, so I decided to begin this by relieving Mr McColl of some of the outrageous number of items on his shelves

I started with chocolate. Apart from the Marxist analysis, there were two other reasons for this. One was that I liked chocolate and the other was that Janet Ralston and I had reached an agreement that I could feel one of her embryonic breasts in exchange for two Mars Bars. Not both her breasts, just the one. The same one every time. I wondered if the other one was the same size. Janet was devious, drove a hard bargain, and it took quite an assortment of Cadbury's products before I was allowed access to both knockers, and even then she refused my perfectly reasonable request to measure them. As Easter approached, and I began to push for some pussy action, Janet's negotiating position became even less flexible. She began demanding pound boxes of Milk Tray for her mother and chocolate eggs for her collection of small snotty brothers, for just a quick butcher's at her fanny. I had decided to take a firmer line with her as she was becoming less desirable. She was putting on weight, which should have hardly have surprised me given the vast amount of Mars Bars she was consuming. I was becoming confused as to whether I was attempting to shag her or fattening her up for the festive season. This was when Harry Taylor entered the equation. He had noticed the chocolate exchanges, and for all I knew, the breast squeezing too. Harry noticed most things; he didn't miss much.

"Where ye gittin' the chocolate fur the fat burd?" he enquired somewhat bluntly. I explained to him my tacit agreement with Mr McColl and he immediately expressed an interest in the arrangement. I was informed that he and Roger Scott would join me as paper boys with the newsagent, assuring me that my present colleagues in the delivery trade were about to resign their positions. I found this highly prescient, as at that point he had no knowledge of who the other paper boys were. But sure enough both had packed in by the end of the week and Harry and Roger were my new co-workers.

Harry had a way of getting what he wanted. Although short and skinny, like many of the Glasgow 'overspill,' he made up in sheer evil what he lacked in physical prowess. At fourteen he was already running an extortion business at school, and had assembled a team of highly talented young shoplifters. He looked upon me as a rival of sorts and Harry had a way of dealing with rivals which no one enjoyed. This inevitably involved a visit to the lavatory with Roger, which was better avoided. In cases of major misdemeanours, it was a visit from one of Harry's four older brothers, any of whom made Roger's company appear almost desirable. His brothers were never seen simultaneously as each was locked up for periods of time in various special schools, borstals, young offenders institutions and, God, the wonder of it all, the eldest was in real jail. This gave Harry the status of demigod. You fell out with him, you fell out with his brothers. Not recommended.

If you didn't agree with Harry under these considerable threats, there was the ultimate fear of an encounter with one of Roger's three sisters, who had lots in common with Harry's brothers, but possessed stronger arms and heavier facial hair. The eldest Leigh-Ann, had recently given birth to a child, and apparently had a ring through her pussy. I was bemused, firstly by the fact that she had a pussy (I was still negotiating with Janet Ralston in that department, so was on shaky ground.) More intriguingly, I wondered how Roger knew the details of the ornamentation of the organ. I occasionally looked at the child and wondered about similarities between the infant and his uncle. Not too often, however, as my imagination couldn't cope with the possibilities that such thoughts initiated.

There were also lesser members of Harry's happy little band, who could be called upon at any time. Basher (I named a cat after him), Plug (not the most glamorous of adolescents), Popeye (a nervous young psychopath with a twitch) and Theresa, Harry's somewhat reluctant moll. And then there was me, quickly elevated to the position of the gang's legal mind, doing everybody's homework and advising on threats and thefts. This position came naturally to me as I was the only one in the gang who could read and write. I was the brains, Roger the brawn. I would tell you what you were due; Roger would turn your face into pulp if you didn't pay. As my fourteenth birthday loomed I was duly joined by the gruesome twosome as my workmates in the newsagent. Harry cased the joint immediately, Cagney style. He watched old Mrs Fisher go through to the back alley as the newspapers arrived, leaving the main shop unattended. She was a trusting soul, Mrs Fisher. Harry could hardly believe what was happening; this was all his dreams come true in one glorious moment. Alone in the front shop of a major store with no one watching. Ah, those glorious years before CCTV. Roger began eating Mars Bars at a furious rate. Harry the business man, prowled around the premises, taking a particular interest in the stockroom. He had the look of a potential stockholder, which indeed wasn't too far from the truth. Only Harry wasn't going to pay for any stock.

Harry, Roger and I concentrated on filling our pockets with various confectionaries from the front shop for over a week, when Harry suddenly stared at me and asked:

"What the fuck are we thinking about?"

I was actually thinking about Janet Ralston's fanny at that moment but I knew this would be the wrong answer and decided to stare blankly back until he informed me what we *were* thinking about.

"That spare delivery bag in the back room!" This apparently was the object of our analysis, although my thoughts were still fixed upon Janet's pubic region.

"What about it?" I enquired tentatively, trying not to appear too stupid.

"Jesus, think about the amount of gear we could get in that."

Thus the spare bag came into the operation. We would fill it every morning with cartons of Bounty Bars, Mars Bars and anything else that we knew would sell. The ice-cream men at the school gates must have wondered why the greedy little bastards who'd been their bread and butter had suddenly gone onto a diet as they watched their sales hit the deck. Surely they couldn't have been reading the Daily Mail which, even in those days, was telling its readers that eating two chocolate buttons a day would lead to imminent death. We enjoyed watching their bemusement.

Business was booming, and Easter was around the corner. With the festival came chocolate eggs, hundreds of the little buggers fitting into the spare bag. As Harry was emptying a pile of them into it one April morning, he suddenly stopped, stared at me, and posed yet another of his unanswerable questions:

"Are we fucking mad?" Had I answered this honestly I would have discussed our dysfunctional families and how the experience of such had left me slightly unbalanced but had inflicted irreparable mental damage not only on him, but on his four delinquent brothers. Instead I once again took the safer option and looked at him with as little expression as possible, awaiting his judgement on what I hoped had not been a rhetorical question. Harry, who was drinking, taking drugs and would have knifed you over the price of a bloody Mars Bar at the age of fourteen, was without question a sandwich short of the picnic. I preferred at that point to define myself as merely slightly disturbed.

He diverted his beady little eyes from me to the wall behind the main counter and shouted "Fags!" in much the same manner as Archimedes must have shrieked "Eureka!" when discovering the secret of hydrostatics. Why were we bothering with stupid sweeties when the place was full of cigarettes? We packed some smokes into the magic bag and went through to the back shop, hoping to discover where the main source was located. This proved more difficult than at first envisioned. As Mrs Fisher continued counting the number of Daily Expresses, Harry and I scoured the entire stock room. Not a carton was found, but what we did notice was a locked door on the wall to our left. Another storeroom. Harry was outraged. The lousy bastards had stashed the main stock of fags in a locked room. We immediately wondered where the key could be. Almost simultaneously I looked at the large bunch of the fuckers attached to the belt holding up Mrs

Fisher's skirt. It was hopeless. The only way into that room would be to remove the belt, which would also get rid of Mrs Fisher's skirt, a move too extreme even for Harry's warped little mind to contemplate. Not only would it be a horrifying experience for all involved, but it would also rather give the game away.

So, although we stole a good deal of fags from the main shop, we had to be rather careful not to make it too obvious. Mrs Fisher was not the most observant woman in life but even she would have noticed if all forty packets of Benson and Hedges had gone from behind the counter before the shop opened. Thus we were forced to continue with the theft of sweets.

It was on a particularly dull, rainy morning in late autumn when I received the unwanted gift that led me into the life of sin and debauchery. As I was leaving the shop on the Monday, carrying the two paper bags, one with the papers, one with a gross of Mars Bars, Mrs Fisher called to me from behind the counter.

"Can I have a word before you go, son?"

Harry and Roger both passed me alarmed looks as they left me with the old lady. Mrs Fisher leaned slowly over the counter and whispered:

"Here's something for your round."

Into my hand she delicately placed a Mars Bar. I thanked her profusely and left with my one hundred and forty-five Mars Bars. Harry and Roger, waiting outside, found this hilarious, but I did not. It affected me so badly that I was compelled to sin without remorse in the future in an attempt to diminish my original transgression. My paternal grandfather was about to explain the concept of sin to me in no uncertain fashion.

MEET THE GRANDPARENTS

My father's parents lived in a tenement flat on the main street of a small coal-mining town in west central Scotland. My grandfather was a retired miner; my grandmother had worked in a bakery after leaving school. Such humble origins, however, in no way affected their overwhelming vanity. They must have been the only mining family in Scotland with a maid. Added to this, she was referred to as 'the maid.' Nothing as prosaic as the cleaner or the home help, but 'the maid.' My parents, my sister and I used to visit them and, as a twelve year old, I was always desperate to see this maid and perhaps order a coffee. Alas it was not to be. Elizabeth must have been a daytime maid or perhaps had Friday nights off, as I never actually met her. Irene, ten years my elder, used to annoy our mother mercilessly, by suggesting we employ a maid too. This, of course, would have been rather odd, given that we stayed in a council house in a new town a few miles from my grandparents. My sister's suggestions that we could be 'a two-maid family,' or that we employ a butler, were greeted by a withering look from my long-suffering mother.

The grandparents' house was, of course, immaculate. (God, it should have been, what with the maid and all!) I remember being in a constant state of confusion about where and when I could wear my shoes. It would have been easier visiting a mosque, but Islam had not been recognised in Cambuslang at that point, and this was a strict Presbyterian household. Born again Christianity was also unfashionable, the grandparents having to settle for the Salvation Army, an organisation in which they had both risen to the rank of general or something equally as grand. The house was full of powerful odours, but the suffocating pong of mothballs permeated the place. No fluttering, lepidopterous insect was going to last long here. My grandparents also smelled strongly of mothballs, in case of a surprise attack when outdoors. 'Never Trust a Moth' was the family motto. The smell of mince, fortunately, counteracted the stink of naphthalene. This was real mince, simmering slowly in a sea of dark brown gravy, and sitting on a black stove fired by real coal. A kind of nineteenth century Aga.

The main feature of the house, however, was the Bible. The holy books were everywhere. In the room where we ate they dominated every free space. Chairs, tables, shelves and stools were all decorated with the holy book. In the parlour, with its *chaise longue* and delicate silk curtains, the theme continued. My grandfather moved them when having guests but they were replaced as soon as the room was vacated. Even the huge incongruous parrot's cage had a Bible next to it, in case the occupant needed some immediate spiritual help. I had a fraught relationship with that bird. We use to stare at each other in silence while my grandfather preached to the rest of the company. I fully expected Polly to recite a chapter of Revelations to me, but she only glared suspiciously, as though she was already aware that I was an irredeemable sinner on a one way path to eternal damnation. This was certainly the view of my paternal grandfather, although, to be fair, he believed everyone to be in this situation. As the early evening light began to fade, he would read passages of the Old Testament to his captive audience assuring them that their ultimate destiny was Hell. I was too young to sin properly but keen to have a bash, as I was apparently doomed anyway.

I remember being overwhelmed by terror one evening when it was suggested that I spend an overnight in the place. As well as the parrot there was Bobby Nairn, the lodger. He sat in the corner of the lounge barely moving. Some Friday nights he would sit with his eyes closed for the entire visit, occasionally adjusting his bunnet to scratch his bald head. He had one arm, with the sleeve of the missing limb tucked into his jacket pocket. He spooked me out more than the bloody parrot. When the overnight stay was mentioned, my seven year old brain went into overdrive in an attempt to avert this fate. I quickly hit the carpet, holding my stomach and screaming in agony. This averted the immediate danger of the 'all-nighter,' but added a new hazard to these dreadful evenings. What if the suggestion reared its ugly head in the future? What new affliction could suddenly attack me? My unease increased dramatically from that point onwards.

Worse was to come, however, when grandpa decided to take me for walks around the town of a summer's evening. Initially I thought that this would be to my benefit, offering an escape from the claustrophobic hell of Mothball House. But now the old man had me completely at his mercy. Damnation was now directed at me personally. I had no one with whom to share the burden of sin. The deadly consequences of my actions were spelled out in great detail. I began to regret pushing John Cameron off his bike or wishing psittacosis on the parrot, which, apart from looking up Sandra Taylor's skirt at school, were the only sins I could think of in these dark moments.

The strangest feature of the walks, however, was the reaction of the townspeople to my grandfather. As they approached us, everyone left the pavement, crossed the road, and passed on the opposite side of the street. This naturally aroused my curiosity, and I asked the old man for an explanation. My grandfather told me that Satan had descended upon the town sometime in the past (he was a bit vague about the date) and had cursed the entire population, apart from him and my granny, who apparently were the only people who believed in God. The rest had sold their souls to the Prince of Darkness and were frightened to confront a blessed one. I noticed that an unusually high proportion of the elderly population were missing a limb or were blind. The town was like night of the living dead. The strange behaviour and blemished appearance of the locals was the Creator's vengeance, according to my grandfather. In my childhood innocence this mindless violence seemed rather superfluous on the part of God, but as he seemed such a nasty bastard at the best of times, I reckoned nothing was beyond him.

It was years later that I discovered the truth surrounding the strange events at the evening promenades. People crossed the street to avoid grandfather because years earlier, about the time the devil had descended on an unsuspecting Cambuslang, there had been a strike in the local pit. As about eighty percent of the town worked there, solidarity was a vital issue, and solidarity was there in buckets. Only one person broke this unity. Nobody would talk to him or share the same pavement. Grandpa was well and truly ostracised in his own community. The missing limbs and blindness of the older men had arrived with World War One or mine explosions, but at the time all of this was beyond my comprehension. I reeled under the threats of eternal damnation, a one-armed man, a psychotic parrot and a town full of zombies.

On Saturday evenings we would visit the house of my maternal grandparents, an entirely different proposition. I had a notion that my mother was on the snobbish side, but when the door of her parents' residence opened I understood what she was distancing herself from. An overwhelming blast of noxious gases spiralled from the house, causing everyone to step aside, as though trying to avoid an evil spirit. The offending wind consisted of a lethal combination of whisky, sherry, wine, dog, cat and human piss, all enveloped in the stink of damp bed linen. Sheet changing was not of a high priority in this household. Bibles had been replaced by bottles. Bottles galore! Hundreds of them! You couldn't move for bottles. Amongst the whisky, rum, brandy gin and sherry, there lay a couple of empty Lucozade bottles, looking as out of place as the parrot had in the other house. My sister would joke that they represented our grandparents' idea of a health drive. Maybe she was correct. They didn't look like the jogging types (although jogging hadn't been invented then either.) Granny Houston would lie sprawled across the sofa, legs akimbo, and knickers round her knees for ventilation purposes, like Hogarth's worst nightmare. Her two remaining front teeth, darkest brown, would overlap her bottom lip, giving her a distinctly Transylvanian quality. She certainly showed a total contempt for the world of dentistry, slobbering softly in a language that was completely alien to me. My mother, on the other hand, seemed to understand all that was being said, nodding her head at what appeared to be appropriate intervals.

The pets were equally intriguing. Two greyhounds and numerous cats wobbled in and out of the room with distinctly unsteady gaits. I suggested to my sister that the animals were also drunk, but this was dismissed as ridiculous. To this day I remain unconvinced. And there was a further problem with the cats. I was unsure that I was seeing the same cats on each visit. I distinctly recall watching a large tabby on one occasion that I had never set eyes on before. I reckoned that the resident cats invited their friends round for a bevy at the week-end.

The highlight of the visit would arrive when Hooky, my step-grandfather, dressed invariably in a 'simmit,' pyjama trousers and braces would arrive with a jar of hair-cream, a brush and a comb. I would then be called upon to perform the weekly hairdressing ritual. He would sit in the centre of the room with a towel wrapped around his neck, his long white hair cascading well over his shoulders. I was required to thump great dollops of cream onto his head before brushing and combing his hair into whatever style took my fancy. Hooky would purr happily as I gave him a middle parting or a straight back. I took a great delight in splattering the excess cream into a basin on the carpet. My mother looked on nervously during this ritual, probably with good reason. Today, Hooky would most likely be on a register.

Mother attempted tirelessly to maintain a position of dignity throughout the ordeal of having delinquent parents. She was the epitome of respectability and sobriety in the town. She neither smoked nor drank, attended church twice a week, and allowed no profanities in the family house. My sister once made the cardinal blunder of using the word 'bloody' over Sunday dinner and was left in no doubt that an eternity of hell and damnation awaited her on the shedding of her mortal coil. When not doing God's work at jumble sales or coffee mornings, mother would frantically clean cupboards and tidy under beds 'in case the minister came.' This always struck me as rather odd. Even if he had come, an event which never took place, why would he want to look under the bed? The minister kept his distance, even though my mother was the ideal parishioner. At every turn she faced defeat. To compliment her dissolute parents, the behaviour of her brother and his sons was fast becoming the talk of the town. Her courageous attempt to become a mixture of Amish, Jehovah's Witness and 'Wee Free' was never going to succeed.

A MAFIA WEDDING

Family life continued in its own unique way. My sister was under strict instructions never to visit our uncle or any of our three cousins and, on pain of death, never to take me near them. My mother feared that our morals would be compromised. She did not approve of her family. We visited each of them often, of course.

My mother's brother, Jack, far from rebelling against his parents, had followed their example, particularly in the field of interior design, liberally decorating his carpets with empty booze bottles. His children, having escaped the family home at the first opportunity, had been replaced with a variety of cats, dogs, snakes and a rabbit, whose home was in a small cupboard under the television. It looked like a food chain in the making, but the animals, picking up on the general lethargy of the place, appeared content to ignore each other and do their own thing. As a younger man, before discovering Smirnoff, Uncle Jack had been an important trades-union official and had travelled extensively in Eastern Europe. As he slobbered at me of an afternoon, in a tongue very similar to that of my maternal grandmother, I thought that perhaps he had picked up one of the Europeans languages and was speaking in Russian or perhaps Hungarian. Drunken Glaswegian is often difficult to decipher. The fact that Jack and his wife, Mary, were both going mad added to the confusion. Jack would mumble to me of an afternoon:

"Ah was a personal friend of Lenin."

I was somewhat confused as to why someone so interested in politics should be close to a member of the Beatles. He was also chummy with someone called Karl Marx, with whom he'd collaborated on a book entitled 'Das Kapital.' I had not the slightest idea to whom he was referring, and for many years later believed Karl Marx to be a woman. Auntie Mary thought that she had been employed as Queen Victoria's representative in Scotland, but had resigned her post to have children. She felt that her three sons should be paying her more attention. I agreed that my cousins were an ungrateful bunch.

Cousin Tom was definitely off limits. Tom and 'that Martha woman,' as my mother referred to his partner, had committed the unforgiveable sin of not marrying. They were East Kilbride's prototype hippies. He had waist long hair; she had flowers in hers. They had children with strange names. Zak and Zoe were titles that my mother did not feel appropriate for the children of earthlings. They smoked cannabis before it became compulsory, and took odd little purple pills which Tom assured me were for headaches. These pills seemed to make them very happy, and the condition appeared infectious. My sister soon developed symptoms which required treatment. She became happy too. I began to feel left out and pined to be struck down with the condition, but apparently, and much to my chagrin, I was too young to have headaches.

Another major threat to our ethical well-being was Cousin Ian, who was also 'living in sin,' but, much to my mother's horror, Ian's partner was called Brian. I liked Brian, particularly when he took me out on his Harley Davidson motorbike. My sister, however, had the unenviable task of explaining the Ian and Brian phenomenon to my mother, who had spotted them holding hands in the town centre and was highly confused by the whole experience. She didn't even hold hands with my father. But two men! It was just inconceivable.

"It's just not natural," she would complain.

The youngest cousin, Robert, had committed the heinous crime of marrying a black woman. "She's not just coloured, she's black," my mother would sob. The fact that the woman was a qualified doctor and a practising Christian did nothing to ease her discomfort. She constantly referred to witch doctors and voodoo, and wondered what colour the babies would be. "D'you think they'll be black or white?" she would enquire, unaware of the probability of mixed race. Orianka should have been my mother's favourite in-law, given that she didn't drink or take drugs *and* believed in God, but the race issue made this proposition a non-starter.

This was the confusing world in which my mother operated. She stood alone, representing traditional family values in the face of this tidal wave of debauchery. She felt a great affinity with my fathers' Salvationist parents, but was burdened with her own heavily tainted blood relations. Therefore much of her time was spent ensuring that the two families would never meet. She had managed this familial apartheid successfully for years, but was suddenly faced with a gigantic challenge. My sister uttered the fateful words:

"Mum, I'm pregnant."

My mother took the news as though she had been informed that she was terminally ill. When she had recovered her balance, she began the immediate interrogation of my sister. "Where did *it* happen?" She presumed *it* had only happened once, and was even holding out for a virgin birth. "Was it in a house? A field? In one of your stupid cousins' houses?" It was the last one that won the vote. Her debauched nephews were behind the pregnancy. Her one crumb of comfort was that the father of the child was Ian Robertson, Irene's childhood sweetheart, who, apart from this dastardly action, actually passed most of mother's horrendous criteria for future sons-in-law. He was at university, training to be a doctor, was from a 'good' family and was not black, homosexual or Roman Catholic. She garbled on for some time about the folly of Irene taking Ian to meet the cousins and how it must 'have turned his head,' changing him into a barbaric sexual predator for a short time. It was only at this point that Irene managed to interrupt the flow and announce hesitatingly that Ian was not the father of the child. Another swooning fit, staring eyes, gushing tears and the fateful words:

"You've no idea who the father is, do you?"

"I'm perfectly aware of the child's father, and we intend to live together as soon as possible. If necessary, and purely to keep you happy, we'll marry."

"Who is he?"

My sister stared blankly at my mother as she prepared to drop the bombshell.

"His name is Paulo Ghatti. He works in an Italian restaurant in Glasgow."

My mother's mouth opened wide at this news and remained agape for what seemed an alarmingly long time. I thought she'd developed lock-jaw. Eventually, her power of speech returned. She looked at my sister in desperation, hoping for a miraculously negative answer to her next question:

"He'll be a Catholic, then?"

Irene answered my mother as though she was a child. Tender but firm.

"Paulo and I have never discussed religion, but as ninety-eight percent of Italy is Catholic, it would seem like a good bet that he might be of that persuasion himself. "And what are we going to tell your father? An Italian Catholic waiter. My God!"

"Wrong on both counts," my sister replied, moving her gaze from floor to wall. "Paulo is Sicilian and he is a chef."

"Waiter! Chef! What's the difference? And what's a Sicilian?"

Irene shifted uneasily in her chair. Mother continued.

"Well you'll have to get married before the bump shows and we'll have to plan it carefully." Her equivalent of the D-Day landings was swinging into operation.

"I'll make the arrangements. You keep quiet. We'll do it in the borders or anywhere away from here."

The wedding was already taking on a criminal persona. It was as though she was planning a bank robbery or a drugs deal.

"The main thing is that you don't tell anyone from my side of the family because they're not going to be there. Is that understood?"

33

The guest list was hardly inspiring, consisting of my father's parents, a few maiden aunts, and two ladies from my mother's church. The bride was allowed three friends and Paulo a best man and one other. Irene's suggestion that my mother might like to meet her future son-in-law before the wedding was reluctantly accepted. She agreed to each of my mother's demands, and the matter was temporarily laid to rest. I had been present throughout, but remained unnoticed, as this was an adult affair and therefore apparently beyond my comprehension.

Two days later cousin Tom sat staring at my sister in his kitchen.

"So you're having a bambino and getting hitched to this Sicilian geezer?"

Everyone except me was smoking the funny smelling cigarettes and taking the headache pills. They were all becoming happy again.

"Why the marriage?" asked Tom. Irene had managed to keep the top secret information unannounced for around twenty minutes, or one funny cigarette and two headache pills.

"Oh, why the Hell not?" replied my sister, lying back on the sofa. I think of it this way. One day's suffering with mother and a few old cronies is a small price to pay for the peace and quiet that will follow. I'm going to need a baby-sitter anyway."

"Poor bambino." Tom shook his head, and took a long draw on a funny cigarette.   "Paulo and his best-man are wearing kilts," my sister added casually.

"Jesus Christ, has the Mafia got a tartan?" replied Tom.

Everyone thought this highly amusing and smoked another funny cigarette to celebrate.

The following week saw the banns posted in Inverness and a venue arranged six miles north of the town for the reception. My sister baulked at this point.

"You couldn't get anywhere more remote?"

"You shouldn't have got pregnant," was the icy reply.

The two women were buzzing around the house awaiting the arrival of the Sicilian. My mother was obviously apprehensive. Her most exotic port of call thus far had been Blackpool and she felt slightly out of her depth with Sicily. As they cleaned the house for the sixth time, she asked my sister a series of ridiculous questions about her fiancé which Irene tried desperately to ignore.

"You do realise that he might kidnap you; that's what they do across there." (She'd been studying Sicilian culture.)

"Listen mother. I asked Paulo out. I made the first move. So why would he want to kidnap me? And who is paying the ransom?"

"Is he in the Mafia? Has he got a gun?"

The stream of questions flowed on until the ring of the doorbell announced the arrival of Al Capone. My mother opened the door to have a huge bouquet of flowers presented to her by an extremely handsome man, who immediately began to shower her with compliments. This continued inside, with Paulo delicately picking up her ornaments and remarking on her exquisite taste. Everything was 'bella' or 'multo bene.' He shot a glance at Irene every few moments as if looking for a critique of his performance. She gestured to him to calm down. She was worried about overacting, but Paulo had certainly struck the right chord and soon the conversation came round to 'the big day.' Instead of this being an under the carpet job, it had turned into a traditional Scottish wedding."I was saying to Irene, we're just inviting our closest friends, so if you could keep your guest-list to perhaps five or six, I think that would do." Paulo's entourage had trebled in thirty minutes. He'd made an instant impression and the secret wedding was well underway. Six weeks later Irene and her bridegroom married in Inverness Registry Office. The assembled company must have made a most peculiar sight on their way to the hotel for the reception, the grandparents and maiden aunts mingling uneasily with Paulo and his small company of Sicilians, who were trying desperately to stop the wind exposing what was underneath their Mafia kilts. Paulo looked only slightly less ridiculous than his best man, whose five foot frame was totally subsumed by a kilt which was at least two sizes too large. He appeared to be wearing an ill-fitting tartan dress.

Castle Lochmore, where the reception took place was an impressive sight. Sitting in a beautiful sheltered spot on the banks of Loch Ness, it really appeared to be, as the brochure stated, 'The premier location for a marriage in Scotland.' The wedding party was ushered through the manicured gardens of the castle on a cold, sunny autumn day, accompanied by the traditional skirl of the piper. Mother had gone the full distance to impress, money apparently being of no consequence. I was beginning to worry about my promised Christmas bike.

The guests were shown into the 'Adam style' drawing room where they were fed vol-au-vents and other things on sticks deemed appropriate for such joyous occasions. The five Italians were finding communication difficult, partly because of their limited English, but mainly due to an obsession with their sporrans. They fingered them continuously, turning them upside down and squeezing them as though expecting a tune to burst forth from the little pouches. Before the wedding meal there was a tour of the castle to be undertaken. The guide, a grossly overweight man in his fifties, tried to look interested as he led the group through the chambers and dungeons complete with torture equipment and, as a novelty, mummified cats. It was then on to the banquet hall for the meal. The menu was entirely Scottish, a warning shot to the assembled Mafiosi that my sister was not about to be 'Sicilianised' too easily. After the starter of Scotch broth, there was a choice of Scottish salmon, Aberdeen Angus or haggis. The Italians all went for the haggis, which offered them another out-of-body experience. They poked their haggis, prodded them, turned them upside down, everything except swallow them. Paulo, being a chef, spent ten minutes asking Irene what constituents made up the dish. My sister spent ten minutes not telling him. The cutting of the cake and the speeches went off with only a minor hiccup, when the best man congratulated the couple on their forthcoming new arrival. My sister, who was translating, hesitated for a second, before adjusting his good wishes to something less likely to offend the maiden aunts and the grandparents. Oddly enough, my mother had omitted to make the joyous news public.

Soon it was entertainment time. Mother's choice again, and she had really gone wild with her selection. The George Chisholm String Quartet consisted of George on violin, a man who appeared to be desperately ill on trumpet and clarinet, a twenty-five stone woman on double bass and vocals, and an emaciated old lady sitting at the harp, looking as though she'd played with the Austwitch orchestra. Their combined age must have been over three hundred and they stared at the audience in much the same way as the mummified cats had earlier. The fireworks began with a waltz by Strauss for the happy couple to begin the dancing. Unfortunately, this was to be the highlight of the performance, it being followed by 'Jesu, Joy of Man's Desiring,' always guaranteed to get any party off with a bang. The grandparents applauded politely, the maiden aunts purred contentedly, whilst Irene and the Italians looked on, completely bemused. 'The Arrival of the Queen of Sheba' preceded 'Stanley's Trumpet Voluntary' and 'The Twenty Third Psalm.' Fearing that 'The Last Post' would be next on the agenda, Irene approached the band leader, suggesting something slightly more contemporary, before the wine took effect and an international incident occurred. There followed a strangulated rendition of 'All You Need is Love' before normal service was resumed.

It was during a particularly prolonged rendition of 'Ave Maria' that the first sounds of trouble could be heard from outside the function room. Raised voices and demands for entry caused George Chisholm and his fellow octogenarians to lay down their instruments, and the maiden aunts to stare at each other in alarm. Suddenly, the door burst open and my mother's vision of Hell poured into the room. It was her parents, Uncle Jack, Auntie Mary, and the three wayward cousins with partners and friends. All were extremely drunk, my grandfather in an open-necked white shirt covered in whisky stains, Cousin Tom with a joint hanging loosely from his bottom lip. Each carried at least one bottle of liquor and had emergency supplies protruding from jackets and handbags. Worse was to come, however, as two of the new arrivals dragged a strange-looking object towards the stage. The maiden aunts looked on in terror. They had never heard of, let alone seen, a Karaoke machine. The George Chisholm Quartet, grasping their instruments to their chests, beat a hasty retreat at this point, accompanied by the encouraging words of Grandpa Hooky, as he began assembling the Karaoke:

"Aye, fuck off you lot. You were crap anyway. Now, seeing it's my only grand-daughter's wedding we're all going to have a wee party."

Speech over, he stumbled across the dance floor, grabbed my sister and whisked her from her chair. Irene, as stunned as the rest of the original party, soon found herself being whirled around the floor to the discordant sound of my cousin Tom's version of Nina Sky's immortal 'Move Ya Body.' The second song saw the unruly relation's wives and girlfriends inviting the Sicilians to dance. The latter, now charged with gallons of wine and released from the agony of George Chisholm, readily accepted. My mother, still open-mouthed at the invasion, responded to her drunken father's invitation to dance with a plea to no-one in particular to phone the police. The maiden aunts furiously declined to take the dance-floor to the strains of my Ian's partner Martha giving her all to Shaggy's 'Hey Sexy Lady.' Martha made sure that the audience understood every nuance of the lyrics. It was all too much for my paternal grandfather, who grabbed the microphone and began a diatribe about the devil's music, being sung by the spawn of Satan.

He was quickly despatched to be replaced by one of the Italians performing a medley of Que Sera Sera, Volare and other classics of that genre. The bride, now also the worse for wine, accompanied the soloist whilst attempting an impromptu striptease. The groom, his fellow countrymen and the party-crashers were all enjoying the show. The local police and hotel security staff, however, were less impressed and began the removal of the interlopers. The stage show was brought to a sudden end as the happy couple, the Sicilians and the intruders were escorted to various police vehicles. The maiden aunts, their friends, my parents and the paternal grandparents sat in the deserted function room staring at each other in silence.

George Chisholm and his musicians had long escaped, leaving only the sounds of embarrassed coughing. The silence was eventually broken by my grandfather who, clutching his bible, suggested that the remaining members of the party should retire to be ready for Sunday service. "We have many souls to ask for the Lord's forgiveness tomorrow," he stated, looking skywards for inspiration. The remains of the wedding party concurred unanimously and made their way slowly to their bedrooms.

SCHOOLDAYS WERE MURDER

Before being expelled from secondary school, I stayed alone with mother. My sister had gone to Sicily shortly after the birth of her child, my father had died, and mother, like her husband's parents, had taken up religion. No one visited the house. The place was cloaked in a deadly silence as mother had decided to stop speaking to everyone, including me. It was also extremely dark as the curtains were never opened. She had adopted the lifestyle of a mole and I had become a reluctant molette. School initially seemed like a viable alternative to the large coffin I called home. At least there was a chance of a conversation there. Little did I realise that it was to be with a murderer.

The school had an air of normality about it. Nothing of any great note happened there. It had never won any major awards, its most notable old boy being a professional footballer. Just a new town education factory where a small percentage of the pupils became managers or accountants, but most became parents, nurses, shop assistants and factory workers. Life continued with an inevitable predictability: the playground fights, the first romances, the dreadful school plays and the interminable science lessons. With the arrival of Tom Dow, however, everyone's life was about to change, none more so than that of Jack MacKay.

Tom Dow was a colossal youth. He joined us in second year, as the rougher kids were forming into gangs and the more studious into little friendship groups. Tom Dow did neither. He *was* a gang; a one-man gang with no one else invited. He stood at around six foot tall, with massive shoulders and thighs like giant redwoods. Most of us were fascinated by him, as though he was an exhibition in a freak show. No one could quite fathom what we were doing in the same class as someone who dwarfed most of our fathers. There were the inevitable rumours that his folks were Gypsies and he had missed a few years schooling, but that alone did not explain the massive height and weight differences.

Dow, however, was no gentle giant. He was, in fact, positively malicious. Whatever had gone amiss in the gene pool to produce this ungainly monster

45

had certainly affected him mentally as well as physically. He was extremely bad news from the moment he strutted through the school gates wearing the unspeakable shirt and scarf. Religious apartheid was the order of the day in the wilderness of west central Scotland and this school was no exception. It was Protestant to the last drop of blood, as the more raucous frequently reminded themselves in song. We were 'up to our knees in feinan blood, surrender and you die.' We were proddies and willing to make the ultimate sacrifice. None of us had the vaguest notion of what a Protestant was, but it definitely appeared to involve hating Catholics, the latter being distinguishable by their red hair and freckles. They also attended something called a chapel, where they performed barbaric acts, often involving animals, and led by someone called the Pope, who was Satan's emissary on earth. However, the most evil manifestation of Catholicism came in the form of their football team, Celtic, who were handpicked by the Antichrist himself and often had the audacity to beat Rangers, who were God's representatives on the planet. Apart from that, we knew nothing about Catholics.

You might imagine, therefore, our dismay when Tom Dow arrived on his first day at school proudly sporting the horrendous green and white Celtic strip, with accompanying scarf tied casually around his waist. This was tantamount to declaring war on the entire 'student body.' The rougher girls complained vehemently to the harder boys.

"This is bloody ridiculous. Somethin's gonnae have to be done aboot this."

Harry and his cohorts were the obvious candidates for the job but our leader instructed us to make no move in this direction. So the gang kept their distance from the new monster in our midst. We were also in an uneasy truce with Davie Robertson. Prior to the arrival of Goliath, Davie had been the school's main freelance hard man. It was left to him to confront this far from jolly green giant. Davie had a big reputation to maintain with any potential male rivals and lots of young *Mademoiselles* to impress. He therefore somewhat hesitatingly approached the monster. "Right you! Get that strip aff, ya feinan bas...."

This David and Goliath battle ended rather differently from its Old Testament equivalent, however. The expletive fizzled out lamely as Dow's eyes pierced down upon Robertson. Then, feigning to turn away, the giant suddenly swivelled round and, with all his considerable force, crashed his huge head full into his adversary's face. The erstwhile champion hard man hit the concrete with a sickening thud, blood pouring from mouth and nose. Dow looked down disdainfully at his victim, casually lit a cigarette, and stared at the stunned audience. "Anybody else like to make a comment on my gear?" Far from commenting on Dow's taste in *haute couture*, most of us were having difficulty breathing. This was taking the world of violence to a deeper, darker place, somewhere we had as yet not visited. Dow, in that single action, had established himself as the new big daddy of the school. No one was in any doubt about that. Even Harry decided to give him a body swerve. Harry was more interested in hard cash.

Dow now set about the task of choosing some victims to torture, allotting them carefully chosen roles. After consultation with Harry, he chose some

48

richer kids to supply him with money and any clothes he fancied, coercing them to steal from their parents. (It wasn't easy being the progeny of the *nouveau riche* at that place. If it wasn't Harry and the hoodlums fleecing you, it was this new monster.) The poorer creatures were subject to various forms of physical abuse ranging from a hard slap in passing to a vicious boot between the legs. Pamela Robertson became his far from willing *amour.* As usual my role, being one of the brighter sparks, was to provide him with copies of any homework we were assigned. I often wondered why none of the teachers questioned the fact that Dow and I did identical work and received identical marks for every subject on the curriculum. Even the English essays agreed in every detail. We did the same things on holidays, had the same uncle and aunt, explored the exact same beaches, and had the same misadventures. Perhaps the teachers had become as circumspect of Dow as his fellow pupils were.

Jack Mackay, however, was chosen for special treatment. This was another puzzle that no one could quite understand. Prior to Dow's arrival, Mackay had, up until this point, been an unobtrusive figure, keeping himself to himself and having no particular enemies. The arrival of Dow soon changed that state of affairs. He took an immediate, unfathomable dislike to Jack. From the first day there began a series of physical and mental attacks, the kicking, punching and extortion being a mere prelude to a constant barrage of sexual humiliation. Jack was forced to remove his underwear, before being subjected to torrents of ridicule about the size of his penis. Dow had a list of insults relating to Jack's private parts. The attacks continued daily from August through to December, the relentless torture cloaked in a veil of silence, like most things in that violent place.

A few days before school broke for Christmas I visited Jack and found him sitting in his bedroom, staring at a box of Black Magic chocolates. The room was in semi-darkness; Jack was deep in thought. Beside the chocolates lay a nail file, a small tube of glue and a roll of Christmas wrapping paper. I attempted to view this as normal, although I was obviously intrigued by the purpose of the objects next to the sweets. Jack had a strange distant glint in his eyes, which made the whole scene even more surreal.

"Are these for your mum, Jack?" I enquired chirpily, knowing all the while that they had nothing to do with his mother.

"Nope." His eyes remained determinedly fixed on the chocolates. I was fast realising that all was not well with my friend.

"Who are they for then?"

"Who do you think they're for?" he replied icily, still staring at the box.

"Jack," I said resignedly, "I don't know what you're doing, but if these sweets are for Dow, I think you should forget it. Giving him chocolates is not going to make him a better person, and you'll only lose what self-respect you've got left."

I was also staring at this point, but not at the chocolates – at the nail file, the glue and the wrapping paper. He looked up at me after a few moments and said very calmly and quietly:

"They are special chocolates - *specially* for Dow."

The last phrase contained a malice I'd never imagined Jack was capable of. He stared at me for a few moments, before walking slowly to the corner of the room, opening a drawer and returning with a large hypodermic needle. He then beckoned me to follow him to the bathroom where he began examining the various bottles on display.

"What kind of after-shave do you think he'll like? 'Brut' probably - he's that sort of guy."

At this, he deftly extracted a tiny drop of the after-shave from the bottle, transferring it to the hypodermic with an expertise which suggested he'd been practising the manoeuvre for some time.

"Now perfume. Christmas just wouldn't be the same without a drop of scent." He leered up at me looking positively possessed as he picked his way through his sister's collection of fragrances.

"Ah, to Hell with the expense, a drop of Chanel No 5." This was quickly followed by: "Oh God, I nearly missed that one!"

He let out a demonic laugh as he showed me the name of the perfume that he was dipping the tip of the syringe into. It was called 'Poison.'

The process continued with a drop of nail varnish remover, a touch of shampoo, and a spot of hair dye. I watched increasingly fascinated as he went about his work with a childlike zeal. Next stop was the kitchen where bleach, window-cleaner and turpentine were added. Operations culminated in his father's garage with a heady cocktail of weed killer, de-icer and paint remover. The vial was by now almost full, but not quite. His last act was to urinate into a cup and transfer a dribble of piss to the hypodermic. He then invited me to contribute a dribble which I duly did. I wondered if I could be done for murder on the strength of a drop of piss, but by that time my powers of rational thought were distinctly on the wane. I followed Jack back to the bedroom in a dreamlike state. The 'Black Magic' box sat on the table as though waiting our return.

"Now comes the tricky bit," he said in a matter of fact voice, as though he was doing a puzzle or threading a needle. He used the nail file very delicately to begin the separation of the thin line of gold paper which held together the two pieces of Cellophane on the outside of the box. Soon we were face to face with the chocolates. He looked at me enquiringly.

"What d'you think he'll eat first?"

"I hope this is not serious," I replied, becoming more alarmed by the second. Even though my involvement with Taylor and the gang had introduced me to the nefarious side of life, Harry, to the best of my knowledge, had not bumped anyone off to that point. Completely ignoring my remark, he lifted the needle and began injecting the chocolates. *Making them special for Dow.* Every soft sweet in the box got the treatment. The coffee-creams, the cherry-cups, the raspberry-whirls. Everything that would readily accept the needle received a shot of the mixture. Only the caramels were exempted, and this merely because he did not want to damage the needle. With the vial empty, he rewrapped the chocolates with the same meticulous care he'd taken to open them and covered the finished article with Christmas paper, depicting Santa and his reindeer.

Next day, at the morning break, Jack, who had begun hiding out during recreation times, appeared in the playground holding the box. Dow immediately descended upon him.

"What's with the Christmas crap?" he growled. Dow grabbed the box and ripped off the paper. He stared at his victim for a few moments, but the chocolates were apparently enough to merit a day off from the beatings. He left, already guzzling his first few sweets. Jack looked across at me but I quickly averted my eyes, pretending to be interested in some other business.

****

School resumed again after the break and things sunk quickly back into the monotonous regime of old. There had of course been the momentous announcement of the sudden, inexplicable death of our fellow student, the deeply missed Tom Dow, with an as yet undiagnosed but particularly lethal form of food poisoning. This caused quite a hullabaloo at the first morning break, with groups of pupils excitedly speculating on the exact cause of the monster's demise. All except Jack, who sat alone by the perimeter fence. As I approached him I noticed he was eating sweets. He smiled at me as I sat down next to him.

"Chocolate?"

He offered me the box. I stared at him blankly.

"They're very nice…… Black Magic."

At this he smiled again adding:

" Don't look so worried, have a caramel.

WORK – A CREEPY EXPERIENCE

Looking at myself in the bathroom mirror, I was suddenly sick. I managed to twirl around and deposit most of the vomit into the toilet bowl, but threw up again on the hall carpet. My first week of work had not been a great success. I had just spent a good part of Friday night and Saturday morning staggering over eight miles through the roughest parts of a threatening city and the deepest and darkest of moors to reach home. I threw up again and again in my bedroom until my stomach ached. Sitting on the edge of the bed, I examined the contents of the basin. At least the puke was mine. The other stuff, coating my hair and congealed into my blood stained jacket belonged to someone else. Someone I was never going to forget. I crawled back to the bathroom and, standing under the shower, watched as the water washed away the debris of the previous night. Scraps of sick joined pink rivulets, tainted by the cuts on my neck and shoulders. I closed my eyes, hoping that when I opened them that I'd had been in a particularly grisly nightmare. The sight of my crumpled bloodstained clothes on the bathroom floor assured me that this was no dream. This was the real thing.

The previous Monday had found me standing outside the offices of Oxide batteries, where I was to begin work as a Trainee Sales Representative. I knew nothing about work (at seventeen this was my first job), nothing about batteries, and had never sold anything legal in my life. I was therefore rather surprised to find myself staring at this ancient, decaying sandstone building in the poorest part of the east-end of the city. It was separated from a line of crumbling slum tenements by a piece of vacant ground, covered in empty wine, cider, and sherry bottles, filthy clothing, mountains of cigarette ends and a collection of needles too blunt for further use. I looked for rats, but they must have been resting. The slums, crying out for demolition, emitted a stench of rancid fat, as their occupants began the daily ritual of frying breakfast for themselves and their progeny. I stood stock-still listening to the slum people shouting at their children.

"Eat that, ya spoilt bastard. Aye and yer goin' tae the school. There's fuck all wrang wi' ye."

A new day had dawned in the shanty town. I looked at my watch. Ten to nine. Time to show face in the battery place. I joined a stream of weary looking souls making their way to the offices. I had no great illusions about my job, but it was going to keep me off the streets until something more appealing appeared. Immediately on entering the foyer I was met by Andrew, whose position I was to fill. He'd achieved some kind of promotion. We had a week in which Andrew was to show me the nuts and bolts of his job, before he left with his parents for a week's winter's break. I felt uneasy about Andrew even at this inaugural meeting. He must have been at least in his mid-thirties, still in a job that apparently could be done by a seventeen year old, and was going on holiday with his parents.

Perhaps these details meant nothing, but Andrew made me feel less than comfortable from the start. He was long, thin, and prematurely bald, retaining only wisps of fine hair at the sides and back of the head, when it really would have been easier on the eye just to have shaved the lot off. It was becoming trendy to be shaven headed by that time, anyway. Looking at Andrew, however, I realised that here was someone who was not concerned with fashion. He was wearing a shiny checked jacket with patches on the elbows, guaranteeing fifty years usage. His brown trousers shone from over-use, as they fought a war of colour with his black scuffed shoes.

The oddest thing about the scenario, however, was that as we marched around the various offices and warehouses, it became apparent that Andrew was somehow in tune with the rest of the staff. Everyone was dressed as though they were extras in a fifties movie. Most of the older women wore their hair in tight buns and had dresses which ran down to their ankles. The younger girls had discreet blouses buttoned up to their necks. The men in senior positions were in conservative dark suits; the younger males had corduroy jackets and sensible slacks. I was happy that I was wearing one of my late father's outfits. Initially I had thought I looked

59

ridiculous in it, but somehow it seemed entirely appropriate for the occasion. It fitted in with the ancient ambience of the place.

After the offices, I was taken to the chilly, badly lit warehouses. Little men in blue overalls scurried here and there, in the cold, shadowy isles, loading batteries onto trolleys or replenishing vacant spaces with new consignments. Every action was completed in the same eerie silence as had been evident in the offices. Next to the gloomy storerooms was the charging shop, manned by an ancient creature who could have been there since the invention of the battery. He wished me all the best, hoping that the Lord would deliver me from evil and protect me from temptation. Before the old man could expand on the message, however, he was harshly interrupted by Andrew with a brusque:
"Right, that's enough for now, dad."
Silence followed, broken only by the quiet clicking of the charging batteries.

The senior members of staff were introduced last, and were just as archaic as their underlings. The head of sales was a huge creature who sprawled behind his desk, a cigarette dangling from his spongy lips. He sucked down the smoke exhaling through his pink, bulbous nose. His office, which had once been cream, was now nicotine brown. Miss Beasley, the accountant, was straight out of Agatha Christie, with her grey hair tied tightly in a bun and her steely blue eyes peering from behind rimless spectacles. The managing director was an ancient man, with a deeply wrinkled face. He resembled a character from a Dickens novel as he leaned over his desk, magnifying glass in hand. He mumbled a brief greeting, before dismissing Andrew with a curt wave of his wrinkled hand.

I had moved from the land of the zombies to the place where time stood still. In this world of odd, aged, silent people, Andrew seemed to me almost run of the mill. This, however, was an impression that was to prove highly inaccurate as the week progressed. I was soon to find his lascivious glances and increasingly personal questions went well beyond the limits of pleasant conversation. His series of intimate enquiries made were far from discrete, culminating in whether or not I was still a virgin. Andrew was not only proud of his own virginity, but disappointed that I had not waited until 'the big day.' Agnes and Andrew had decided to wait until their wedding night before consummating their relationship.

These matters, however, were to be discussed in more detail on Thursday, when the three of us were to have lunch at Agnes's house. I was far from enthused with this idea, but, on the other hand, had decided to humour him for the time being. I spent the next three days following him around the offices and warehouses of Oxide batteries like a pet dog, through rooms of silence, broken only by the ring of the telephone, the click-clack of a typewriter, or the warning bleep of a fork-lift truck reversing. The few conversations I had with my mentor inevitably ended in disagreement. We were diametrically opposed to each other on practically every issue on God's earth, including the existence of the Supreme Being himself. I soon noticed that Andrew was becoming increasingly impatient with his pupil, referring to me as 'stupid' and 'ignorant.' When I suggested that such descriptors were somewhat less than Christian, the response was a shrug and a positively menacing, 'Agnes will sort you out, young man!' This threat seemed to imply physical violence. I dreamt of being thrown into a deep pond by the pair, to ascertain whether or not I would float, the victim of some witchcraft trial. The fiendish duo then dragged me out of the water, their twisted faces smiling insanely as they prepared to burn me at the stake. I awoke covered in sweat, wondering what was to follow. This was before I'd even met Agnes.

Thursday arrived. At twelve we walked round to her house for lunch. Agnes stayed nearby the Oxide ghetto, but upwind of the stench of the slums. She was exactly how I had imagined her: hair in bun, two-piece suit, sensible sturdy shoes and an anorak partially hiding her expansive body. The house was barely furnished, and uncomfortably cold. I immediately realised that this was to be more of an extended reprimand than a lunch. Over watery soup and thin sandwiches she grilled me about my views on abortion. 'Andrew tells me you are in favour of killing babies.' Next it was homosexuality. 'You do realise that indulgence in unnatural sex leads irrevocably to an eternity in Hell.' Politics and religion followed. 'Andrew tells me you're a bit of a communist as well as an atheist.' I had mentioned under pressure that my relations were on the political left and that I sometimes doubted, looking at the mess the planet was in, whether a benign creator really existed. Something had got lost in translation.

The inquisition dragged on for almost an hour. My life of dissipation was juxtaposed against her own selflessness, and that of that of the morally impeccable Andrew. They not only led sinless lives, but rescued others, day and night. I stared at her cold bespectacled eyes, as she droned on about her work with the Girl Guides and her doting fiancé's deeds with the Boy's Brigade. I envisaged the huge woman going through the sexual act with her scrawny partner on 'the first night,' Andrew gasping for breath as she thudded up and down on his scrawny frame. I wondered if he'd be wearing his jacket and slacks and she her anorak, as they prayed for forgiveness while fornicating. He would pay for any sin he had inadvertently committed on that occasion. I was tempted to tell them about Roger's sister and the fanny ring, and inform Agnes where she could get the work done, perhaps suggesting that Andrew have one in his dick, but I felt outnumbered and rather scared. The faultless pair and God were against me. At least there had only been one holy parrot in my earlier encounter with the Supreme Being.

On and on she garbled. After saving the souls of the nation's youth of an evening, the relentless do-gooders fed the local down and outs in the soup kitchen they operated near the battery place. I hoped the soup was more substantial than the flavoured water I'd just endured, or there would be some mighty hungry vagrants wandering the wastelands. I was invited to join their order, the Church of Ultimate Redemption, but demurred politely. I had, however, to join in a prayer before leaving. Agnes, bible in hand, beseeched the Lord to reveal himself as soon as possible, before Satan took her young guest's soul to the fires of hell. The 'young guest' was more than grateful to return to the relatively benign iciness of the battery factory, rather than freezing to death in Agnes's holy hospice.

Friday, the day before his departure, Andrew confronted with me an offer I really should have refused, but mistakes were being made by the dozen at this point, and this was to prove my last and most disastrous. He informed me that there was still a deal of information I had yet to be shown about my new post, suggesting that I stay for a few hours at the end of the day to complete the basic training. I thought it best to concur. Having thus far given the impression of being Satan's son, I felt that I should attempt some damage repair.

Standing at the gate of the battery place on the Friday evening, I watched the office girls discussing their choice of clubs as they vanished into the gloom of the winter's night. The warehousemen followed closely behind, heading for the nearest watering hole. I felt increasingly uneasy at having agreed to spend hours in the company offices alone with Andrew. My thoughts were interrupted as my mentor arrived and, much to my astonishment, suggested that we have a drink in the local pub before beginning the last part of the training. I readily agreed. Anything was better than more of the bloody batteries.

On entering the dingy overcrowded bar at the corner of the street, I expressed my surprise at Andrew having a drink. He laughed loudly, saying that he had a pint only rarely, and no harm would be done as long as Agnes did not get to know his little secret. The bar was packed full of battery men, jostling for drinks and shouting, even though they were packed together like tinned sardines. I stared at them from a corner seat, thinking how strange the contrast in the behaviour of the workers after their week of silence in the warehouses. It was as though a Trappist monastery had turned into a football crowd in the space of an hour.

Andrew asked me what I'd like to drink. I shouted over the cacophony that I'd have a pint of lager, and, although I initially declined, also took a proffered whisky. The spirits, when they arrived, were larger than I'd expected. Much larger. I looked at Andrew suspiciously as he smiled, holding his glass near his cheek and shouting 'bottoms up.' The two of us downed his whisky in one gulp. I tried desperately not to cough as the drink burned into me. I gulped the lager in an attempt to calm my throat, as Andrew excused himself for a toilet break. No sooner was he gone, than he returned with another two massive whiskies. Another 'bottoms up' and it was down the hatch again. I was not sure why I was doing this. Initially it had been to prove my willingness to be cooperative; now it was as though I was trying to assert my maturity. I was even smoking cigarettes, a habit I'd previously avoided. Drinks arrived with the monotony of a conveyor belt. I wondered how Saint Agnes would feel about this Bacchalian orgy.

The evening progressed, with Andrew insisting on buying all the drinks. I became extremely drunk and more than a little confused. The conversation advanced from work to the physical attributes of each of the office girls. Andrew, although still stressing the danger of sex before marriage, had apparently given the act plenty of thought. At around nine he suggested that we go back to the battery place so that I could pick up the work documents and look them over at the week-end. We left the pub and re-entered the world of the tenements once more. A light snow swirled around the buildings as we approached the battery warehouses. They loomed up through the gathering gloom, threatening my already shaken stability. I wished I was elsewhere. Anywhere. Suddenly Andrew stopped at an old, decaying house next to the main gates. He took a key from his pocket and casually opened the door. Even with the numbing effect of the alcohol, I was becoming more than a little alarmed. I had noticed this place during my week at the factory, but thought it deserted. There were some threadbare curtains partially covering the cracked windows of the house, but I had never noticed any light coming from the building. Andrew beckoned me reassuringly. "Come in, this is where the files are."

I entered the living-room. There was an abominable stink, which I attributed to the various empty liquor bottles and used milk cartons covering the floor and table. I thought of my maternal grandparents. Sagging brown wallpaper hung desperately to three of the walls, the fourth playing host to a grimy window, under which stood a huge scum encrusted sink, full of unwashed dishes. I was fascinated by the sink. Why was it the same room that they presumably ate and watched television? But who were *they*? And where was the television? Not having a T.V. was unthinkable in my environment. "Make yourself at home. Have a seat," Andrew said, in a tone rather too intimate for my liking. He was leering at me in a fashion that was now positively disturbing. I watched as he poured another two large whiskies, before producing a tin, from which he took a lump of cannabis and a packet of cigarette papers. This was Jekyll and Hyde in high intensity.

"This how you and Agnes relax after saving the souls of the needy?" I couldn't resist a touch of sarcasm. His tone changed immediately.

"Mention anything of this and I'll make sure you regret it," he replied menacingly, as he began rolling a joint.

"No offence. I'll not tell if you don't." This seemed to relax the host a little.

"Now, the reason for all this violence..." Andrew, much to my discomfort, had been in the middle of a protracted monologue about crime in the east end, before leaving the pub. "The real problem with crime is that the courts are too soft on the bastards who offend. Agnes and I live in a constant state of terror in case what happened to Trevor might befall us."

I took a drag on the joint against my better judgement. Any sensible options open to me were now fading fast, and I was deeply confused as to why I was there. The idea of studying the work files had become a distant memory, and the time to catch the last bus was fast approaching. But I was transfixed by the dual personality of this strange

70

creature sitting across from me. Mr Hyde was definitely in the ascendancy.

"Trevor was attacked in the next street on his way to visit me last month. He needed over fifty stitches in his face alone. Look at this." Suddenly, he produced a photograph album from a paper rack next to his chair. I watched in amazement and with a good deal of trepidation as my increasingly strange host turned the pages with a fanatical enthusiasm. Each page contained an image of a horribly mutilated young man, whose face was totally disfigured by a succession of huge scars. Disturbing white foam bubbled at the sides of Andrew's mouth as he closed the album. "Now what would you do with the vermin who were responsible for ruining that beautiful boy's face. Personally I'd incarcerate them in my basement, and torture them in total darkness for the rest of their lives. I'd cut off various parts of their bodies like their fingers and toes, but I'd keep them alive for as long as possible to watch them writhing in agony."

He finished the rant and stared hard at me, looking for a reaction. I gazed back at the contorted

71

face and the thin line of foam coursing slowly down the chin. By now I was frozen in fear, thinking about making a bolt for the door. This was much more than I'd bargained for and I wanted out.

"Who took the pictures?" I could hardly enunciate the words.

Andrew smiled, and leaning across towards me, said slowly and softly:

"I did, of course. Do you like my photography? I have a certificate."

"Peculiar subject matter," I said, attempting to hide the tremor in my voice. Anyway, I need a pee after all this excitement. Where's the toilet?"

"Just do it in the sink. The stair light's out and the flush is broken."

The sink was against the wall with the tattered curtain. As I urinated, I felt a presence behind me and turned sharply to find Andrew peering over my shoulder.

"Watch your aim now. I'm just going to hang up our coats. You might as well stay here tonight. The snow's coming down thick and fast. You can sleep in my parents' room."

I stumbled back to the sofa, checking my watch on the way. Christ! I'd missed the last bus and didn't have enough for a taxi. It was going to be a long night with this madman in his asylum. When my host reappeared, I informed him that the drinks and drugs had taken their toll, and it was time for me to hit the sack. Andrew was less than pleased about my decision, and without as much as looking at me, stated curtly:

"Your room is first right at the top of the stairs."

I walked slowly to the hall and flicked the stair light. A seedy orange glow lit up the shabby stair carpet. It produced a faint glow but, contrary to Andrew's earlier assertions, it *did* work. The light in the parents' bedroom did not, and I was left to undress in darkness. I kept my trousers on, partly because the room was extremely cold and partly....well, something told me to leave them on.

The room smelled like death. I remembered keeping the body of a small dead bird that I had found as a child until it began to decompose. The stench in this room reminded me of that odour. The stink of the damp sheets provoked a feeling of intense nausea, but the effects of the drink and drugs were kicking in, and my eyelids soon closed. They were open again immediately, as I was

73

grabbed from behind by a pair of very powerful arms, which held me in a full-nelson. A voice muttered words about 'cock-teasing' and 'getting what you came for.' I could hear Bob Dylan's 'Visions of Joanna' coming faintly from the living room as flashes of the photographs and the scum in the sink flared into my vision. My attacker's hard penis was thudding against my trousers as he scratched and bit at my neck. I could smell the alcohol and tobacco on his hot breath, as he removed one of his arms in an attempt to open his trousers. Gasping for air, I realised that this was my chance to halt the onslaught, and, with all the strength I could muster, crashed my free right arm backwards into his ribcage, causing him to groan and temporarily loosen the grip of his other arm. At this I battered both elbows into his solar plexus. I heard a piercing scream behind me, as Andrew emptied the contents of his stomach over my head.

I stumbled from the bed, quickly collecting my jacket and shoes and ran down the stairs, accompanied by a wailing sound, as a distressed naked Andrew stumbled from the bedroom and, losing his balance, fell head first down the steep stairs, landing in a pool of blood and vomit at my feet. The injured, bloodied figure stared up at me and croaked: "Forgive me. I didn't mean to harm you. I'm not even homosexual. It's Agnes you see, she won't let me do it until we're married. It's driving me insane."

He held his bloodied head in his hands and began howling. I wiped some of the vomit from my hair and face, finished tying my shoe laces, and looked at the prostrate figure on the floor. I drew my right leg back and smashed my foot into his face. The blood poured from his mouth and nose. His whining had been replaced by a deep gurgle which soon ceased after I kicked him again. Andrew now lay peacefully at the bottom of the stairs. I walked slowly back into the living-room and picked up the photo album of his scarred and mutilated friend and emptied the photographs over his face. The bloodied images merged quite exquisitely with the crumpled, bleeding mess that became their host. I kicked him again, between the legs, hoping for a response, but he only juddered slightly under the impact. I was hoping that he would have some time to compare his own rearranged face with that of his young friend, but thought that it might be a while before that took place.

I slept until mid-afternoon on Saturday. Waking, I wondered down to the kitchen, and made myself a sandwich. The phone rang. It was a friend. I arranged to meet that evening, explaining that I had an important letter to write, which I wanted to do when events were still clear in my mind. 'Dear Agnes,' the letter began. It was better that she knew now, rather than later; perhaps it could be the start of a conversation on their wedding night. Who knows? I can't recount the exact outcome as I decided the life of a Sales Rep was not for me.

STARTING LINES, FINISHING LINES

After my encounter with Andrew I decided that a change of career might be in order. Perhaps I'd be better suited to an outdoor occupation. I took a job back in the ghost town of my birth, painting lines on the roads. White lines down the centre, yellow lines at the kerb and, occasionally, on a rainy day, a bus shelter or two in battleship grey. My colleagues were the two Jimmies. Not everyone from the west of Scotland is called Jimmy, but these two certainly were. Jimmy the painter and wee Jimmy, the painter's labourer. I had no title as such, being referred to in the third person by Jimmy the painter as 'that fucking peasant,' inevitably via wee Jimmy, as in 'Jimmy, tell that fucking peasant to bring the paint over here.' The peasant title, I presumed, related to the way I dressed, particularly the straw hat, which Jimmy found unbearably offensive, and completely beyond belief when I embellished it with a pheasant's feather. On seeing this for the first time, Jimmy's face contorted into so many agonising shapes that I thought he was going to be physically sick. However, he contented himself with a loud 'Jesus Fucking Christ' and went about his business.

I didn't wear the straw hat specifically to annoy Jimmy, merely to stop my nose and forehead burning in the sun, but his reaction did come as a bit of a bonus. Anyway, I *did* wear the feather to bug the old bastard, and had many abusive titles for him, invariably delivered at a safe distance.

Jimmy was an aggressive character, an explosion in the Second World War having left him with a metal plate in his head, which I always took to be a replacement for that part of the brain which deals with rational thought. It wasn't only me that Jimmy hated. He detested almost all life on earth. He would spend the hot summer days bent over the line-painting machine cursing women, children, cats, dogs, horses, poofs, pakis, niggers, refugees, lefties, students, social security scroungers, writers, and painters (but not road painters.) The list was endless, usually culminating in a rave against his wife, who was a 'frigid cow.'

I was designated a poof student. When I protested my innocence on both charges, his eyes went from mine to the feather in my hat and back. Nothing was said. The feather spoke for itself. I was definitely a poof. My newly found position as a student had an equally obvious explanation. 'Well, look at your fucking hair. You must be a student.' Apparently, anyone with above average hair length was at university. We used to pass hairy tramps and drunks lying in the gutters of the roads we were painting, and I would ask Jimmy if they were students. "Aye, they're fuckin' students, too lazy to fuckin' work, and ah pay ma taxes so that these bastards can get bevied. Probably fuckin' poofs as well." I didn't like the tramps joining me as a 'poof student.' It seemed to diminish my newly found status, but Jimmy refused further discussion of the matter. My course studies were also defined by Jimmy. When asked what I was doing at Cambridge, he immediately replied, "Readin' books, that's what poofs do at that place." I felt oddly flattered that I'd risen from being an unemployable lout to this bright, gay chappie reading books at the university, although still a bit miffed about sharing my quarters with the booze-slugging, hairy tramps.

Jimmy also was a keen analyst of sexual behaviour in the animal world. As I sat reading the paper one sunny afternoon, he glanced at a headline. "What's that all about?" The article concerned a horse which, after winning 'The Triple Crown', had changed ownership for a million pounds. Jimmy's response to this was unusual, but given his thought processes, perhaps predictable. "Fucking Hell, a million quid for a horse!" I explained it was for breeding purposes but this was dismissed as ridiculous as the horse was "probably a poof anyway." I tried to explain that the likelihood of homosexuality in the equine world was somewhat minimal but Jimmy stuck to his guns. Nijinsky was gay.

It was when Jimmy's sidekick decided to get on my case that I lost my sense of humour. On a grey, drizzly morning, with the roads too wet to paint, wee Jimmy and I were sent off to paint bus shelters on a dual-carriageway. As we finished the first and I sat down with my coffee (poofish) to read the Sporting Chronicle (not poofish), I noticed that wee Jimmy was pacing nervously up and down the shelter, passing me the odd hostile glance. Unknown to me, Jimmy was about to ascertain his position in the food chain. The rain had changed from a light drizzle to an all-out downpour as Jimmy broke what had been a long, awkward silence.

"Right, Ken, we're going to paint that shelter over the road. Bring the trestle and the paint tins."

I looked at the rain. It was coming down in sheets. You could hardly see the bus shelter which Jimmy had chosen, and would be likely to suffer death by drowning in any foolhardy attempt to reach it.

"Okay, Jimmy, I'll see you across there when the rain stops."

"Get the paint in the trestle and get moving, arsehole." Wee Jimmy had suddenly turned into my boss.

"Fuck off and paint the thing yourself." I was fast reaching breaking point with the two Jimmies.

Little Jimmy stretched to his full five feet two inches and declared:

"Listen you, you smug bastard, Jimmy's the painter, I'm the painter's labourer and you're the painter's labourer's labourer."

Later in life, when I *was* a student, I learned the academic term for falling off the career ladder. It was called 'downwardly socially mobile,' and often applied to company directors who'd hit the bottle. The decline into destitution could take years but I'd managed to plummet from being a top gay student at Cambridge University to a painter's labourer's labourer in one day. Surely some kind of record.

However, life became increasingly more difficult after the bus shelter showdown. Jimmy the painter became physical. Everything I did he found unsatisfactory, resulting in a kick at least. The verbal abuse intensified, but it was the physical attacks that bothered me most. I decided to reply in kind with something that Jimmy would not forget, supposing that his memory was still functioning in his metal head.

I resigned from the position but retained my interest in Jimmy the painter. For weeks after leaving the job I watched Jimmy's movements carefully. He was extremely predictable, particularly at the end of the working day. He'd pack his brushes carefully, putting each in its allotted place in his leather shoulder bag. He then took the same path back to his frigid wife, a route which included a narrow track between a park and his house. It was there I waited for him until one evening we were alone. He walked slowly towards me, head down, mumbling threats

82

against some section of the population. I wondered if it might be me, but brushed that aside. Jimmy would have forgotten about me by this time. He was about to get an unpleasant jolt to his memory. "Hi Jimmy," I said loudly as I approached him. It was to be the last thing he'd hear before I smashed my hammer into his head. I gave him another crack as he fell to his knees. There was a fountain of blood, but, much to my disappointment, a chilling lack of sound. I'd given a lot of thought to the weapon which was going to wipe this particular turd of the face of the earth and was really interested in the metal plate in his head. I expected a kind of clanging sound as metal met metal, but only got a quiet crunch as the hammer landed on the skull. The old bastard had even denied me the pleasure of a proper groan, just letting out a small squeak as he hit the ground. Andrew's demise in the battery house had been much more satisfactory than this debacle. More noise, plenty of groans. I thought of laying into his face which stared lifelessly up at me, but it was in such a mess that I decided I couldn't make it any worse. I stuck a Mars Bar into his bleeding mouth and moved quickly away from the scene.

ANOTHER JOB - ONE THAT TOOK THE BISCUIT

Braithwaite was a torturer. In another age he would have punished non-believers by the twist of metal, the tightening of bonds or the lash of a whip. In that hell-hole masquerading as a biscuit factory, he had to devise more subtle ways of satisfying his sadistic urges. He was, moreover, the boss and could choose the methods of humiliation that best suited him. He chose his victims carefully, only the most vulnerable meriting his attention. Harper and Jackson were two of his favourites. I was also considered a suitable candidate for treatment. I had recently completed a short prison sentence, not for Andrew or Jimmy, but for what I considered a minor affray. The judge had taken a dim view of the knife, which I hadn't even used. The other two were in a similar situation, forcing us to put up with whatever crap Braithwaite threw at us.

The boss man was fully aware of the situation, and had made up his mind to exploit it. Being young and foolish we decided to take him on, a situation the older man thrived upon. It suited him perfectly. He enjoyed breaking people, sucking out their last vestiges of resistance. Failure to make this job work would probably mean another stretch behind bars for the three of us, so the night manager felt he could basically do as he wished. We endured the monster's attention every night, planning revenge for a future date. It was only when he turned his attention to Ian that we decided that the day of retaliation had to be brought forward. Ian was our constant companion as the nights turned to weeks, the weeks to months, and the half-covered biscuits descended upon us in their millions from the chocolate room above. The night shift only baked and packed the one type of biscuit, chocolate digestives, although it was known from some slick detective work that the twilight and day shifts made other biscuits. We longed to make another biscuit: a bourbon maybe, a jammie dodger, or a custard cream. But there was never any respite from the ubiquitous half-covered digestives. In an odd way Ian kept us sane in this mad world, although he was quite bonkers himself. I always wondered at what point he had lost his sanity; was it overnight, packing one biscuit too many, or had the relentless march of the chocolate digestives driven him slowly crazy, chewing inexorably at his grip on reality over a period of years? Either way, the boy had lost the plot and had exchanged his own miserable existence with that of an altogether more exciting alter ego. He was a frightening sight, leaning over the packaging line with his crooked frame and his sleepy eye. Looking at Ian conjured up images of bells and a Parisian cathedral. Ian was unlikely to win any beauty contests but had a marvellous saving grace. His fantastic stories stopped us dying of boredom and kept us alive through the endless nights. His imagination made Jules Verne appear dull. Unfortunately, Braithwaite had noticed this too and decided to put a halt to things before anyone started enjoying the long night-shifts.

Monday nights were always the worst, but Ian inevitably came to the rescue. The poor trapped creatures around him could depend on him to lighten their load. Just a simple, 'What did you do at the weekend Ian?' and the fun would begin. To hell with Tolkien, this guy could really do fantasy, and to add to this he always researched his subject matter enough as to lend a sense of realism to the stories.

When he told you that he had dined at the most expensive restaurant in the city, he would produce a copy of the menu, and discuss the merits of the chef. He had an odd air of plausibility about him. This, however, quickly vanished when he discussed his imaginary girlfriend, Charlotte, a girl of some social standing in the local community. When talking of Charlotte any semblance to reality took a major backseat. One Monday Ian informed me that he'd taken her ski-ing at the weekend. When I asked him where he replied nonchalantly, "oh, just locally." As the only pieces of raised ground near where we stayed were two disused slagheaps, and Charlotte was a lady of expensive tastes, it must have been somewhat disappointing, not to mention uncomfortable, for the poor girl. He occasionally slipped up with Charlotte.

This particular week had started as usual with Ian doing a spot of painting. 'D'you remember I told you my favourite artist was Van Gogh.' Ian was a fan of Vincent, but also a critic. He was especially critical of the sunflowers, which apparently did not have enough colours. Ian painted flowers too, but his were more vibrant. He had also informed me that Van

Gogh had got pissed one night and had bitten his own ear off. Ian had by now started his own series of self-portraits. I gulped hard on hearing this information, remembering Van Gogh's face as it became more insanely tortured with each of the self-portraits. Had Vincent managed another three he would probably have brought off a good likeness of Ian, with his alien head, Spocklike ears, sleepy eye, and crooked teeth. I couldn't decide on the scariest scenario; Van Gogh actually biting his own ear off or Ian's self-portrait. I checked Ian's ears; there were still two

The nights continued to drag on with the biscuits flooding down from the chocolate room in their millions. Ian's procrastinations on life would blend in with the clatter of machinery in the great mechanical zoo. But Braithwaite was always there, hovering over us like an avenging angel. At one point he acquired a stopwatch, which pleased him immensely. Fifteen minutes were allowed for breaks, not one second more. Braithwaite and the stopwatch made sure of this. Even the factory cat was subject to his strict interpretation of the regulations. Arriving in the grain store one morning he suddenly realised that he was a minute early. He stared at the assembled company, and then at the cat.

"What's he doing?" he asked, staring at the animal, who was half-way through a corned-beef sandwich.

"He's having a sandwich," Ian replied helpfully. We knew by the older man's glare that the innocent remark would have heavy consequences.

"Don't you think his time would be more profitably spent catching mice?"

Even the cat was on time and motion.

On returning to the conveyor line, Ian decided to leave the subject of art, which was beginning to confuse his workmates. He changed to politics. He'd touched on this briefly the previous week, so had had time to let his imagination come up with a few ideas. No one was going to be disappointed.

"What are you going to vote, Ian?" asked Jackson, a committed communist.

"Er... I'm not going to vote."

Well this was certainly a first. But he wasn't getting off too easily. The biscuits were bugging his fellow packers. They needed entertainment.

"Why not?" said Jackson

"It's too dangerous."

"Too dangerous? Why's it too dangerous?"

Ian beckoned Jackson and Harper to come nearer. They leaned across the conveyor belt. The biscuits started tipping off the end of the line into a large bucket. He looked to his left and right, and then whispered a phrase which thoroughly confused them. They stared at him quizzically, as he conveyed some top secret information. Unfortunately, the clamour of the machinery made it impossible to hear him accurately.

Harper looked across at me, shouting:

"He says he's a troglodyte. What the fuck's a troglodyte?"

"Someone who lives in a cave," I offered helpfully.

Harper turned back to Ian.

"I know you're a head banger, but why the fuck are you staying in a cave? Did your mother throw you out? Tell her you're sorry and she'll let you back. You can't stay in a cave, you'll catch something."

This was only partly heard by Ian, and by now they were both staring at each other curiously. We were all sinking in a sea of chocolate digestives as everyone had stopped to hear about Ian's cave-dwelling.

"I said I'm a Trotskyite," he shouted at the top of his voice. "Why are you going on about caves? Trotsky, like me, believed in world-wide revolution, but I've got to watch what I say. I'm a member of a political party but it's banned so I can't talk about it at all. I've already been arrested and tortured. They take you to Skye where they've got a huge torture chamber under the hills."

"Why did they torture you Ian?" I asked. By this time there were biscuits everywhere, but Ian was in full flow, which was worth a lot more to his audience than some lousy half-covereds.

"Because I know too much."

"What d'you know?"

He smiled at me, his good eye twinkling, and his sleepy one focused on the floor.

"Now I'm not going to tell you that. You could be a government agent."

I stared at him, a grave look on my face.

"That's the bad news, Ian. I am a government agent, sent here on a mission to root out Trotskyites from biscuit factories. You are under arrest. There's a car outside, you're going back to Skye. We can to it peacefully or the other way. It's up to you."

He looked at me with genuine fear on his face, his functioning eye twitching furiously. It was only when I assured him that I too was a Trotskyite that the night resumed an air of normality, if talking of torture chambers in the Cuillins while up to your waist in chocolate biscuits can be viewed as in any way normal. By now the packing area floor was a positive swamp of half covered digestives. The dark side of this little episode was that Braithwaite had taken time off his cost-efficiency exercise with the cat to watch the whole scene from behind the packaging machine. He appeared like an apparition, and, with a gesture of the hand, beckoned Ian to follow him. The two marched in silence to the dreaded chocolate room, Ian a few paces behind the tyrant.

I had taken to wandering around the factory during my breaks, walking amongst the giant ovens where the process began, watching the half-cooked dough being emptied into the giant hoppers, ready for transportation to the conveyor belts, the chocolate room, the final cook, the coolers and ultimately to me, where they were dressed in their shiny suits, ready for the stores. The conveyor belts, ovens and packing machinery were all fairly straightforward but the chocolate room was something entirely different. Outsiders were not allowed up the restricted staircase to this mysterious place. Only if you had eighty years service could you enter this holy of holies. The Sikhs had their Golden Temple, the Catholics the Vatican City – this was the biscuit world's equivalent. I vowed to gain entry at any cost, obsessed by the secrecy surrounding the place. Why were only a privileged few allowed access? Were they doing experiments up there? Was Mengele still alive? Ian's imagination had begun to rub off on me.

Then, out of the blue, I found myself not only in the chocolate room but working as the chocolate man. I was standing one night listening to another of Aesop's fables when all hell broke loose. Auld Jock and his companion, who had been the chocolate men since the time that my auntie Mary had been Queen Victoria's lady-in-waiting, had been involved in a car crash and were presently in hospital, being examined by a taxidermist. Panic ensued! The biscuits were still on the march and the chocolate room was unmanned. Suddenly I was grabbed by Braithwaite who, with a crazed look in his eyes,

93

ordered me to follow him. Up the stairs we rushed, all the way to the chocolate room, where I was handed a very large metal fork. I had become the chocolate man. Never have I felt so proud, before or since. I knew how Hilary must have felt on the summit of Everest, Armstrong on the moon. Braithwaite handed me a giant fork, rushed off, and left me standing with the implement dangling by my side. I had no idea what to do with the thing. As I watched the half-covereds emerging from their chocolate bath, I noticed that occasionally one of them would jump on top of another one (well I suppose it happens after a bath sometimes.) I felt that I had some strange moral obligation to put a halt to this behaviour and separated the lascivious biscuits with my large fork. This, I decided, was the purpose of my presence in the chocolate room.

Mary Whitehouse was popular at the time as a moral campaigner and somehow I had become her representative in the biscuit factory, showing the chocolate biscuits the true path, keeping them on the straight and narrow. My behaviour was beginning to make Ian's ravings seem like a treatise on rationality. There was about fifty tonnes of metal in the chocolate room alone, but I decided that the whole process could be stopped by one biscuit mounting another one. Looking back, it does appears somewhat irrational, but, as no-one had given me alternative instructions, I went with my original idea. I watched carefully for wayward digestives.

Thirty minutes passed with only one coupling. I decided to help them along by placing one biscuit on top of another for a few seconds, before separating them again. I was feeling the heat. The chocolate room was beginning to get to me. I viewed the place as a kind of pre-Hell, a purgatory where I'd been sent to ask God to forgive me for my sins. The intense heat was taking a heavy toll on my thought processes. I began to feel extremely dizzy. After forty five minutes I tried the door. It refused to open; the maniac had locked me in this pressure cooker. Another fifteen minutes of sweating profusely, and in a state of near collapse, Braithwaite appeared and I was freed. I staggered outside in a state of complete dehydration, my skin burning, my lungs on fire.

.

My condition, however, had given Braithwaite food for thought. He watched us every minute of every shift after this, screaming at us if we transcribed his rules by an inch, rules which varied according to his moods. Punishments were many and diverse. The slightest speck of dirt on a fingernail, a hairnet not at the exact angle, a trace of tobacco smoke would incur the monster's wrath. And suddenly the chocolate room had widened his sadistic options. He had noticed the mess an hour in the chocolate room had made of me, and began to use it as a punishment chamber for his other slaves too. What had began as an emergency had widened the sadist's horizons. He had a new toy with which to torment us. An hour in the room became the standard punishment for any minor misdemeanour.

He also had the back-breaking hopper. Thirty minutes on this could drain the life out of the most rebellious of creatures. The hopper men were exclusively huge West Indian or Eastern European creatures with massive arms and gigantic thighs. They had the most exhausting job in the plant, moving the half-baked dough in metal baths from the giant ovens at the far end of the factory to the

96

conveyor lines and the packaging area. What made the hopperman's task so unique was the consistency of the mix he handled. The dough at this point was soggy and clinging. It stuck to the baths, reluctant to leave, forcing the huge hoppermen to plough frantically at it with their wooden-handled blades. Their great frames glistened with sweat as they dug at the mixture throughout the night, their only source of relief being when Braithwaite would send them a victim they could mock for an hour. No normal mortals could do the job of the hoppermen, and they were fully aware of this. An hour on the hopper would see the average worker return to his station physically and mentally wrecked. All of us on the packaging line had experienced the hell of the hopper except Ian - even a sadist like Braithwaite seemed reluctant to subject someone so lightly built to a spell on the hopper.

The chocolate room, however, was deemed to be within his range. Ian's first sentence to the place was greeted with an eerie silence. We all wondered how the frail creature would cope. He staggered back to the packing area an hour later in a state of complete disarray, only vaguely aware of his surroundings. We brought him water and towels and eventually he came back to consciousness - at least to Ian's form of consciousness. He'd been damaged mentally as well as exhausted physically. His chastisements in the chocolate-room took place regularly after the first night, but they did not curb his story-telling. His wild tales began to balloon out of all proportion after his first session. His stories became more disjointed and surreal. He began having ridiculous weekends with the beautiful Charlotte in which, after wining and dining her in top Parisian restaurants, he would regularly save her from rape, attempted murder, and frequent kidnapping attempts. He flew to exotic destinations with her every weekend, where crazed foreigners had to be fought off every ten minutes. When I asked him where all the cash was coming from to finance these adventures he had an immediate answer.

"Money doesn't matter to me," he said with a straight face. "I inherited a fortune from my uncle. He was a tea planter in India. Owned the whole of Typhoo."

"Handy," I replied.

"Damn right," he said casually, as though inheriting millions from a tea planting uncle was an everyday event. "By the way, I'm going to paint Charlotte next week......naked." I had a momentary vision of the girl covered in Dulux Brilliant White with a blue and white Saltire on her head but managed, as in the case of Rodger's sister's sex life, to banish the thoughts to the back of my mind.

It was shortly after this artistic moment that the unthinkable happened. Ian arrived uncharacteristically late, and Braithwaite grabbed the opportunity to march him off to the hopper. We watched in reverential silence as he was lead to his punishment, terror in his eyes at the thought of the mountains of soggy dough in their metal baths awaiting him. To nobody's surprise Ian did not last long at the Hopper. He was stretchered to an ambulance after twenty minutes, watched by most of the workers. Braithwaite was noticeable by his absence, but at that moment something had changed. He no longer followed our every move, he stopped overtly stalking us, and was seen less around the factory. But we took more interest in the supervisor. We tracked his movements each night. A

99

few weeks after Ian's injury we knew his nightly routine. The hunter had become the hunted, retribution time was drawing near It seemed that Braithwaite was aware of this, his manoeuvres becoming distinctly more circumspect, his presence less noticeable.

The plan was hatched shortly after a delegation from the factory had visited Ian in hospital. The patient was recovering slowly but it was obvious to those who saw him that he would not be returning to work. There were no more stories, no wild anecdotes, and it seemed that even Charlotte had ceased to exist. We discussed what to do about Ian's tormentor at the break that night. His punishment was set for two o'clock the following Saturday morning. We could specify the time from our extensive investigations into Braithwaite's movements since Ian's injury. Production halted for routine maintenance each Friday night at midnight for two hours to allow cleaning and inspection of the machines. It was at during this time that Braithwaite toured his domain, prowling around the almost deserted factory, staring lovingly at the packing machinery, the conveyor belts, the chocolate room and the place where the process all began, the cavernous hall above the gigantic ovens where the tons of flour were mixed with malt and hundreds of gallons of water, all of which constituted a single batch of digestives. It was here that Braithwaite finished his tour each Saturday morning, and it was here that he was to pay for his sadism.

As he stood alone peering into one of his beloved ovens, five of his slaves approached him from behind. Harper covered his head with a flour sack as the rest of us began pounding him with heads, fists and feet. The figure under the sack fumbled and squealed for a few moments before suddenly falling limp and lifeless. We stared at each other through the half-light of the grain room before hastily removing the sack. There was no movement in the eyes of the blood splattered face that met our gaze. Panic descended on the assailants. Nobody had meant to kill Braithwaite, just injure him as badly as he had Ian.

"What'll we do now? The fucker's dead," a nervous voice muttered from the back of the group. Harper, as always, kept calm.

"Right, the old bastard has had a heart attack. Too bad. What we concentrate on now is not getting caught, which means getting rid of the body.

"How do we do that?" Another voice from the gloom. By this time, however, all eyes were on the giant oven against which was slumped the lifeless, battered corpse of Braithwaite.

"If this thing can cook 1500 pounds of dough in the next few hours then this fat bastard is not going to make a lot of difference to the finished product. He loved the fucking things, now he can be part of them. Fuck him!" Harper had solved the problem. We lifted the body onto the rim of the oven, and, with an almighty push, despatched it through the gaping hole down into the dark world where it came to rest next to the huge blades which would presently churn it alongside the other ingredients of the digestive mixture. I threw in a Mars Bar to sweeten the recipe. He had been a bitter man, Braithwaite, and I hoped the chocolate would sweeten his journey to Hell.

The first batch of the new line of half-covered digestives slowly emerged from the chocolate room at around five that morning. As they approached the packaging line we looked at each other nervously.

Each of us let the initial biscuits pass by and roll onto the floor. It was left to Harper to break the spell.

"Come on," he said, almost cheerily, "let's taste the new biscuits. They're usually at their best just after a good clean out." He picked one from the line and took a bite. We nervously followed suit and soon everyone was munching on a chocolate digestive. Well, there was really no one there to stop us. The biscuit I ate tasted like any other chocolate digestive, although, just for a moment, I imagined that I had detected a hint of nicotine on my tongue. Sheer fantasy, of course, but I've never eaten a chocolate digestive since. I stick to Mars Bars.

UNIVERSITY—A SPOT OF UPWARD SOCIAL MOBILITY

I'd had enough of work and decided to try a spot of education. I fucked around for a year or two and was accepted to University on the grounds that I was old. My first morning was spent sitting in one of the lecture theatres. Next to me, glowing with good health, dripping with ostentatious wealth, sat one of the most beautiful women I'd ever seen. From the fur coat and the diamond rings to the pearl necklace and brooch, she positively oozed affluence. I'd moved up in the world and this company was much more to my liking. The scent of my immediate neighbour helped me forget the stink of the grandmother's house, the paint and the chocolate digestives. The dean began his introductory speech.

"You are about to enter a unique new world where the past will mean nothing. A world of egalitarianism where you will be judged solely on your performance from this point onwards. There will be no favouritism and no favourites. You will all start from the same place."

I looked at the fur coat and diamonds and had an odd feeling that, even with his reassurances, the

Dean was talking through his arsehole. In a mile handicap she would be giving me furlong start. This feeling was heightened when the time came to fill in the enrolment forms. I had a moment of difficulty remembering the name of my secondary school – it had been quite a while ago, and I'd only attended in order to do some trading in stolen goods. She had no such problems. I surreptitiously watched her as she boldly printed 'The Mary Erskine' with her silver Parker pen. The name of the school intrigued me. The Mary Erskine. I'd never heard of a school whose title began with 'The.' It sounded like a ship to my unsophisticated ears.

Speech and form filling over, the Mary Erskine picked up her handbag and made her way to the exit. I followed at a discreet distance, making sure there was always a few people between us. At the student café she ordered a cappuccino and took it to a window seat near the corner. Still tracking her, I bought a regular coffee and sat at an adjacent table. I watched her closely as she produced a small mirror from her bag and examined her perfect face, making sure that everything was immaculate. It was flawless down to the last eyelash. She delicately sipped her coffee and discretely puffed on a Black Sobraine, taking care not to inhale. Looking around, her gaze eventually descended on me. I quickly looked away.

Giggles and shrieks were the order of the day for the other students. Young girls in tight blouses invited others to join hot-air balloon clubs, architectural digs, and drama groups. Young chaps enjoined other adolescents to become members of the rugby club, the Liberal Democrats or the debating society. Believers cajoled everyone to enrol in bible classes and hear the Word of the Lord. The sons and daughters of the ruling classes were celebrating another step in their progression to the leadership of society.

I was having difficulty understanding what was being said in this torrent of gushing enthusiasm, partly because of the volume of the bright young things and partly because of their accents. I hadn't realised until then that people actually used such words as 'daaaling' and 'ya' in every day speech. The Mary Erskine did not share my curiosity, waving away the youngsters with a flick of her Sobraine and a withering look. I wondered if she would understand me, should I ever find the courage to engage her in conversation. I doubted this very much, resigning myself to watching her on the far horizon. A majestic craft that would never be boarded. The Mary Erskine.

I wondered what 'the Mary' would make of the man I was going to visit. I had not seen nor heard of my father for many years, yet this week I'd been overwhelmed by a strange desire to meet him. God knows why. Maybe it was because I'd heard he was still alive and living in the same house. I wondered what The Mary Erskine would have thought of this world I was entering - a world I was certain she would never have dipped her toe in.

I began the walk from the city centre to the east end. The Top Shops and Boots were soon replaced by Asian grocers, bookies, and clandestine drug dealers lurking on street corners. I was quickly surrounded by high intensity housing, with graffiti scarring the claustrophobic tower blocks. The slogans on the walls invited niggers and Pakis to fuck off. A solution had been given to the natives to explain their dilemma. Soon it would be the Romanians and Bulgarians to blame, but they were still packing their gear and saying their goodbyes in Sofia and Bucharest. The indigenous population, some thousands of miles west, were preparing to greet them by swallowing pills and downing drugs by the bucketful to escape the reality of life in the promised land. But the area had one thing in common with the nouveau riche. Hardly anyone worked here, so tax payments were not a part of this world. Pacific havens, where the bankers holed out, were rather more pleasant, but essentially operated on similar lines.

I knocked hesitatingly on the door of my childhood home, but there was no reply. I tried the door handle, turned it, and walked into the house. I noticed a sickly sour stench in the hall, but as I entered the living room, the stink was so nauseating that I slumped onto the settee holding a paper handkerchief to my face in an attempt not to be sick. I looked at the stains on the carpet. The rug had once been cream but, with the addition of a cocktail of various wines, spirits, faeces and vomit, it was now terrifyingly multi-coloured. That was the visible parts. Most of it was covered in the detritus of what appeared to be years of drinking. I knew that it represented, at the most, only a few months. I could even tell from the bottles something about his lifestyle. The cheap whisky and vodka meant benefits day. The cheaper gut rot wine and cider implied one or two days before payment time.

108

Suddenly I heard someone cough in the darkest corner of the room. It was only then that I noticed through the gloom that there was a woman sitting at a table in the corner. This lady, however, was not drinking Cappuccino; she was finishing off a bottle of White Lightning cider. I strained my eyes, trying to focus on her. She appeared to be in her late fifties, but with the mask of make-up she was wearing, it was hard to tell. She could have been seventy. Thinning peroxide hair straggled across a deeply furrowed face, which was wet with sweat and cider. Her mascara had spread from her eyes to cover most of her cheeks, and her lipstick had been applied so badly that it reached the base of her nose.

"He's no here, he'll be in the boozers," she slurred, rising unsteadily from her chair and staggering towards me. She sat on the stained carpet, looking up at me imploringly, her garish, painted face assuming a nightmarish quality in the fading light. I wondered what The Mary Erskine was doing that Saturday evening. I heard in the distance the desolate woman's voice. "Listen son. Ah need to get some booze. Could you afford a fiver? Ah'll make it worth your while, like."

109

Looking through the grimy window, I saw the high-rise flats disappearing into the winter's night as the woman unzipped me and took my penis in her mouth. My gaze turned to the photograph on the opposite wall. My mother stared at me from my parents' wedding photograph. I was glad she was dead. Next to it was a faded photograph of Uncle Jack, Auntie Mary and their sons. I became conscious of the woman sucking on my dick. She had removed her false teeth which certainly added another dimension to the experience. I ejaculated into the toothless cavern in silence. The act completed, I gave the woman a ten-pound note. I felt that I had re-entered the world of my youth. The scent of the Mary Erskine had been replaced by the stink of unwashed vagina and stale booze.

"Thanks, you're a pal," she said, heading for the door.

I spoke for the first time since entering the room.

"What's your name?"

"Mary," she replied, grinning slightly, her rotten teeth peering at me through the shadows, a dribble of my cum snaking down her chin. "Nice name, eh?"

I grinned back.

"The Mary....." I said quietly, my thoughts filtering back to the beginning of the week.

The woman looked confused then glanced at the ten-pound note.

"The one and only, babe. Let's you and I get a drink and go back to ma place. Ah think you're in need of a wee bit education."

We walked past crumbling buildings through the ensuing gloom, stopping off at a booze shop where a wary grocer served me a litre of vodka and a bottle of lemonade. Mary's dwelling was a carbon copy of the house we had just vacated. The same torn curtains, hanging desperately to the wall joined by a few nails. The same stink of stale tobacco and booze. The night passed in a blur with the occasional sucking noise issuing from under the odorous blanket. University had started on a low note. In the morning light I viewed the crumpled twisted wreck that had been sucking my dick for a good part of the night, and wondered if university was really for me. On this evidence I was heading for an STD rather than a PHD.

MARRIAGE—NICE PUSSY

It was a particularly dangerous drive back to the village that evening, with the radio warning of hazardous road conditions. One mistake in this hostile terrain could mean deep trouble. Notwithstanding this, I always used the moors road, as there was next to no traffic, and I was invariably pissed and stoned. The only sign of life that evening was the tawny owl which swooped upon the car, attracted by the headlights. The fleeting visitor told me that I was roughly five minutes from my house, five minutes from Catherine, as barren and hostile as the most desolate of moors.

I wondered what awaited me that evening. Catherine usually concentrated on one topic. Perhaps tonight it would be my friends, a favourite and recurring subject. Each of my acquaintances was urgently in need of therapy in Catherine's world. Some were alcoholics, ('Who does she think she's kidding with the Coca Cola? There's a half bottle of vodka in her handbag.') Others were drug addicts. ('If he takes another snort of that stuff, his nose will fall off.') Sexual deviation also figured prominently. ('Who does he think he's fooling with the wedding ring? He's as bent as a boomerang.') She had even hinted at paedophilia for a certain colleague, whom she particularly disliked.

Occupations also came under strict scrutiny. The hairdresser I knew was actually a brothel keeper. ('The only hair he's interested in is pubic hair! Look at him! He's as bald as a coot.') In Catherine's world, baldness meant you were automatically incapable of cutting hair, and the barber's red and white pole signified an invitation to unlimited sexual debauchery. My car-salesman pal only sold vehicles after stealing them and changing their number plates, and my friend with the bookshop.......well, what changed hands under the counter in his place would make your eyes water.

Being her husband, I was the primary target. Amongst other things, my occupation troubled her deeply. There was something not quite fitting in being the wife of someone who worked in a liquor warehouse, even as manager. As the head teacher of a primary school, she occasionally entertained guests from the world of education, and would positively

113

cringe if I as much as mentioned my job. I noticed, however, that this did not stop Catherine and her cronies downing all the booze I could liberate from my workplace. But that was Catherine.

My clothes were another favourite avenue of attack. When casually dressed, I looked like something the cat brought in; when formal, I became a tailor's dummy. My accent and language were also a cause for concern. Although having crawled through university, and spent what seemed like decades listening to Catherine's affected twang, I still retained the vestige of a working class accent, which induced in my wife feelings of uncontrollable nausea. Added to this, I swore! Initially, my profanities were accepted as the natural expression of my uncouth upbringing, but as our relationship deteriorated, I became aware that I was swearing intentionally, with the express purpose of annoying Catherine. This seemed to be particularly effective at her dreary dinner parties.

And of course there was the cat. The cat that could do no wrong. Her beloved Timmy, who was kind, sensitive, lovable and intelligent, indeed everything that I was not. Catherine repeatedly asserted that the cat was brighter than me, until I began to suspect that she actually believed in what she was saying. With each tirade she launched, she would frantically stroke the feline, who appeared to me to be nodding his head in agreement. The cat seemed to totally concur with the character assassinations. When each attack had reached its climax, and Catherine had stormed off to her bedroom, Timmy would look at me disparagingly, hissing and spitting before strutting disdainfully from the room. The cat was beginning to bug me.

I turned into the drive of the cottage and switched off the engine. It had been another hard day at the pub and I was feeling positively groggy. I had not been at work for over four weeks, having obtained a medical certificate for depression. Instead, I had been spending each day at a friend's hotel on the other side of the moor, drinking, playing cards and becoming ever more friendly with Julie, a girl from the local village. She was everything that Catherine was not. She was kind, understanding, and clever. Furthermore, she exuded a sexuality which took me back to my adolescent years. Even more satisfying was that she appeared to find my company pleasing, a feeling I hadn't experienced for quite some time.

However it was not Julie I was about to meet that evening, but the ferocious Catherine, my living nightmare. She started before I had a chance to remove my coat.

"And what the hell have you been doing for the past month?"

Her shrill voice pierced the silence of the room like a blade cutting glass. She sat on the armchair facing the window in the early evening gloom. I could only see her bare elbows, but even they seemed to exude an hostility. My head was spinning from the effects of the afternoon's booze and my deepening relationship with Julie. Thoughts of the new woman, however, were abruptly halted by Catherine's question. How did she know about my recent history? She must have phoned my office.

"I've been feeling too ill to work lately," I stuttered.

"Too ill to work," she spat, "but not too ill to get plastered, you useless bastard."

At this, she stood up, spun round, and delivered the most sustained character assassination that I had endured in years. I was the most inept, useless, futile, impotent individual on God's earth. She had put so much effort into building this perfect life for us, whilst my only contribution had been to swallow and to wallow. Swallow the booze and wallow in the mire of self-pity. I wasn't worth the ground that I stood on, the air that I breathed. And throughout the tirade, she held her beloved Timmy in her arms. The cat that could do no wrong. It stared dismissively at me, apparently agreeing with every word that emanated from the mouth of my relentless antagonist. By now I was convinced that the cat was concurring with all that was spoken. Eventually, Catherine's sea of scorn dried up, and she made her way to the bedroom, leaving me to drink myself to sleep on the sofa.

Morning came up like hell. I groaned quietly, as the various alcohol induced pains shot through my body. Conventional hangovers had long since been replaced by a variety of agonising stabs, each of which acted as a memory enhancer, reminding me that I was sober, a condition which had to be remedied as quickly as possible. As the booze was launching a particularly malevolent attack on my kidneys, Catherine swept into the room, her bright red dress stinging my eyes. Her appearance caused me to feel considerably worse. However, much to my surprise, she appeared almost conciliatory after the previous evening's bombardment. Her tone of voice was disarmingly non-confrontational, almost verging on the pleasant. This left me bewildered, so confused that I offered to buy and cook the evening meal.

"Well just something simple, and try to show your face at work. Oh, and get the cat some food, the expensive stuff that he likes."

Still in a state of puzzlement, I readily agreed to each request. On her departure, I sat at the kitchen table, contemplating Catherine's mellowness, and having my first drink of the day. After much head scratching, I decided that her behaviour was a temporary phenomenon which would rectify itself by the evening. I stood up and stretched, causing the cat to hiss and scurry from the room. I hissed back. It was eight thirty. Two hours later, I found myself propping up at the bar on the other side of the moor, playing cards with the barman and a few locals. Early afternoon saw the arrival of Julie who, after a few drinks, suggested we retreat to her place for 'a bit of privacy.' I had yet to make love to Julie, but given my perilous marital position, and fuelled by the morning's alcohol, I was in no mood to refuse any offer of solace. As I looked lovingly at Julie across the pillow later that afternoon I suddenly remembered the promise I'd made to Catherine. I decided to fulfil my pledge about the meal, but resolved to end the marriage as soon as possible.

On the way back over the moor that day, my mind became so fuddled with the prodigious amount of booze I'd downed and my intimacy with Julie, that I had to pull over to the grass verge to gather my thoughts. This, however, consisted of more drink, which made the remainder of the journey even riskier. Eventually I spotted the tawny, which meant that home was not far away. The patter of rain on the windscreen joined the purr of the engine as I glanced at the clock on the dashboard. Fucking hell, I was cutting it fine. Soon I was staggering from butcher to grocer, making it to the house with thirty minutes to spare before the return of Medusa. I shovelled the mince into a pot with a few stock cubes, before almost cutting a finger off attempting

119

to slice an onion. I dumped the coarsely chopped vegetable into the pot, accompanied by half a cup of water and almost the same amount of blood. After half-heartedly attacking a turnip, and roughly peeling some potatoes, I staggered over to the kitchen table.

With ten minutes to arrival time, I was slumped at the table, staring at the bottle of vodka. It leered back at me provocatively. I had no intention of confronting Catherine with news of my imminent departure, having already decided to do this in a busier location, but the very thought of meeting her that evening had taken on a significance of its own. There was no doubt about it; Catherine scared the shit out of me. Even the bloody cat worried me, but her owner's ambition, pretentiousness, ostentation, and overwhelming self-confidence made me shiver. I had decided on a quieter life; she appeared to have designs on the throne.

Suddenly the noise of a car engine in the drive jolted me out of my depressing reverie. On hearing the door open, I quickly hid the vodka under the table, and sat bolt upright in his chair, feigning sobriety. Catherine stormed into the kitchen,

120

throwing me a disdainful glance. Normal service had been resumed, I surmised. She scrutinized me like a detective assessing a murder suspect.

"Been at work then?" she enquired, removing her coat and throwing it over a chair.

"Yes, I popped in for a few hours this morning," I lied, trying to enunciate each word clearly, hoping this would disguise my intoxication.

Catherine stared menacingly at me for what seemed like an eternity, before walking slowly over to the cooker, where she proceeded to view the contents of the utensils. First, the mince pan. Next the potatoes. All was going well until she uncovered the turnips……then disaster! On removing the lid, she turned towards me, her eyes blazing, screaming at the top of her voice:

"You dirty, stupid, useless moron. This really is the last straw. I'm off, and if I ever see your sorry face again, it'll be a lifetime too soon. I hope you die in agony."

At this, she ran from the room, and there followed a short period of door slamming, and suitcases being dragged from cupboards, every action being accompanied by the foulest of insults, each directed at me.

I lit a cigarette, even though this was strictly *verboten*. I was more than a little confused by the reception given to the turnips, but nothing seemed to matter too much now. Timmy walked passed, hissing, as I slumped across the table. I stared at the animal. With my hands supporting my head, I focused blearily at the pans on the rings of the cooker, particularly at the turnips, which seemed to be the source of this great hullabaloo. I wobbled towards the oven, balancing myself with one hand on a wall, and removed the lid from the mince pan. No problem here, with the mince simmering away contentedly. I tasted the meat. It was fine. I decided to include human blood in future recipes. The potatoes had the same result. No problems. So it was over to the turnips, the dreaded turnips that appeared to hide a horrible secret. I moved to lift the lid on the offending veggies, but stopped abruptly, as though some unseen force was protecting it. I tried again, with the same result. "Open the bloody thing!" I shouted, and with a swift snatch, grabbed the lid and threw it to the floor. Rooted to the spot, I stared in horror at the contents of the pan. A deep brown murky liquid peered back at me. The viscous fluid churned around slowly, emitting the occasional bubble, which would burst and send a cloud of vapour towards my face as my eyes remained transfixed on the hub. The mixture looked extremely poisonous, seeming to possess a strange alien quality, as though it was not from this earth. Nothing, however, could have been further from the truth, as it was composed almost entirely of earth. I had, in my drunken stupor, made the somewhat elementary error of forgetting to peel the turnip, before tossing the large chunks into the pot, where they boiled ominously in their sea of mud, occasionally popping out to spit at me, as though mocking my drunken condition.

I switched the cooker off and resumed my place at the table, beginning another attack on the vodka bottle.

"It was a mistake anyone could have made," I mumbled to myself. A few moments later, after a swift mood change, I was laughing uncontrollably, vodka spilling over the table, over my trousers, and over a deeply distressed cat, who growled viciously at me.

"God, she's left her precious bloody pussy cat," I heard myself slur, as my blurred vision caught a glimpse of the animal, retreating to safer ground.

"How would you like some mince, you fat bastard," I called after the vanishing feline. "Nah, I don't suppose it's posh enough for you."

As a final act of defiance, I stubbed my cigarette out on the hall carpet, shouting:

"How d'you like that, Catherine, my darling. Now I'm going to pour some vodka down my gullet, and the rest on your favourite piece of furniture."

Dawn arrived like thunder next morning. Squinting at a bruised sky from my sofa swamp, I listened in agony to the howling of the cat, the tumultuous crashing of outside doors and the horrific explosions of car engines igniting. This must have been similar to how the residents of Hiroshima felt on the fateful day. I crawled from sofa to carpet, picking up what remained of the vodka on my way to the bathroom for the first pee of the day. The urine was an unhealthy murky brown not unlike the turnip mixture. It emitted a powerful odour informing me that my kidneys were taking industrial action. Carefully avoiding mirrors, I stumbled back to the sofa, sitting down heavily and suddenly realising I needed another pee. Fuck you, I thought, there's no way I'm going back there, I'm not Captain Oates. The birds had joined in the cacophony of unbearable noise, a morning chorus of harpies each aiming its caterwauling screech at a point between my eyes and each scoring a direct hit as I finalised my seated piss. I stared blankly ahead as specks of dust floated downwards, each landing on the carpet with a crash that threatened what was left of my shattered ear drums. Reaching for what remained of the vodka, I used it to wash down a handful of tranquillizers.

Deciding not to cross the moor that day, I spent the morning and early afternoon trawling about the local pubs. My telephone rang once, and I answered it eagerly, thinking it would be Julie. Instead it was Catherine, threatening me with everything short of public execution. She apparently had been having me followed for weeks, and was suing me for divorce on the grounds of physical and mental cruelty, alongside the adultery which, by all accounts, she was well aware of. Furthermore, she intended to bankrupt me, have my employment terminated, and institute proceedings to evict me from the house. In the meantime, I had to make sure that I was not in the aforesaid property at six o'clock that evening, as she was returning for the cat and the remainder of her clothes. Failure to comply with this last request would result in my physical injury, as she was bringing company. Things were turning nasty. Defensive action was necessary but difficult, as I felt as though death was just around the corner.

By five that evening I was once more seated at the kitchen table, muttering incoherently to myself. I had opened yet another bottle of vodka and was swallowing more pills. Deep confusion had long ago taken the place of rational thought; uncertainty was in the ascendancy. I staggered across the kitchen and looked at the turnips. Switching on the cooker, I began heating the potatoes and the turnip sludge on low flames. Then I switched on the oven at a higher temperature. The cat meowed. He hadn't been fed for a day. I emptied some of the mince into his bowl, bent down warily and began patting the animal. As I stroked the cat, I stared at the opposite wall. "Nice pussy...nice pussy." I recited the words over and

126

over again as the cat cautiously nibbled at the meat. Twenty minutes later I was driving erratically over the moor, pop music blaring from the radio.

****

I thought of Catherine driving carefully towards the house at around the same time. She would turn up the radio, in an attempt to drown out the thunder, assuring herself that I'd be out of there by now. The threat of physical violence would have done the trick. Opening the front door, she would stand in the hallway, listening to the silence. Suddenly, she'd become aware of a powerful smell. It was the smell of cooking, perhaps chicken, but is seemed stronger than poultry, and the closer to the kitchen she approached, the more convinced she was that this a different kind of smell. Switching on the kitchen light and almost overcome by the fumes from the oven, she would see a note on the table. She'd pick it up, trembling, almost unable to decipher the message because of her shaking hands. She would read:

127

"Have a nice meal. Hope the turnip gravy enhances the main dish."

Swivelling round to face the cooker, she would feel a horrendous numbness descend upon her, as she sank to her knees, repeatedly screaming "Timmy, Timmy." There would, of course be no reply, the eerie silence broken only by a low spitting sound coming from the oven.

THE HOOVER MAN

Looking into the mirror, I examined my wrinkled face. God, my yesterdays were catching up with me. My once golden hair had become the subject of a takeover bid by an insidious creeping white and the crows feet under my eyes were spreading like the Mississippi delta. The cops had nabbed me for the cat incident and I'd spent a few years in the nuthouse. Still, I'd escaped the nastier crimes of the past so I wasn't complaining. But life was exacting a heavy toll and I'd decided to take things quietly. I'd managed to swing another job in a bar in the outskirts of the ghost town. Another waste of a day in my life awaited in this awful place. Picking up the remains of the previous night's vodka I took a long swig. This was somewhat superfluous as there were gallons of the stuff awaiting my arrival at work but I needed a kick start to see me through another endless day.

. The public house was a vast, gloomy, godforsaken place, with the atmosphere of a morgue. A few tables and chairs seemed to have been dropped at random in the yawning space facing the gantry. A pool table sat by the far window like some kind of afterthought. Alongside, a Wurlitzer jukebox whined out doomed love songs from the sixties. A permanent shadow of dust coated the place, with powdery grime immediately re-establishing itself after dusting. I would stand of a morning imagining what might have happened in this dreadful dive. I usually decided on murder; it seemed the most appropriate. Murder in the morgue. As there were no customers before midday, when a few desultory souls would wander in for a plate of soup and a roll, I spent entire mornings completely alone, wiping imaginary stains from the bar and mixing myself cocktails. All this was about to change, however, with the arrival of the Hoover Man.

He strode in one bitter February morning, rubbing his gigantic paws together, and ordering a pint of the strongest beer on sale with an air of jollity which I found entirely inappropriate given the temperature, the immediate environment and my prevailing mood. I poured the drink and examined my first early-morning customer for several months. He was too

130

jolly to be an alcoholic, so why was he necking pints of the strongest lager at nine-thirty in the morning? The Hoover Man was also grossly overweight, with a huge pink, pockmarked face suggesting that this morning's drink was not his first. His enormous eyes popped out from his face like two loosely connected poached eggs, and his short fat legs struggled to support an enormous stomach that cascaded over his waist like that of a Sumo wrestler. He was certainly not the most impressive of the male gender, but, being my first morning customer for some time, I decided to strike up a conversation with him, a decision I was later to regret deeply.

"What you up to today, sir?" Even as I asked the question, I had the uneasy feeling I was doing the wrong thing.

"Same as I do every day. Fixin' Hoovers. I've never done much else, nor would ever want to. It's the most satisfying job on earth. Ever fixed one yourself? Na, I don't suppose you have."

This last phrase seemed to carry with it a distinct hint of malice, making me wish that there were others in the bar, or that it was situated in a more populous area. I almost apologised for the fact that not only had I never fixed a Hoover, adding that I would probably have some difficulty switching one on.

The Hoover Man stared at me disparagingly, taking a long pull at his pint.

"Listen mate," (the 'mate' was distinctively unfriendly), "if you'd ever done a good job on a Hoover, you'd remember it forever. I once dismantled and reassembled a Dyson DC07 Upright, cable length 8.2 metres, weight 8.7 kilos, 1200 watt, in less than two hours. It was the proudest moment of my life."

We stared at each other in total silence; I was regretting deeply that I'd initiated the conversation. The Hoover Man was quickly revealing himself to be deeply unbalanced. Breathing heavily, his mouth opened and closed like a tropical fish.

" I'll have another pint and one for yourself," he gasped

I wished that this was to be our first and last conversation but knew that this was not going to be the case. The Hoover Man arrived at ten o'clock each morning for the next two weeks, assailing me with tales of his Hoover repairing. Unstoppable and

132

incessant, the hoover stories would gush from his cavernous mouth. I became his stupefied audience, day after day, caught in a vacuum, unable to stop the inexorable flow.

"They call the Kauikis head on the Sebo K range 'deluxe,' but personally I've found the Dyson Flexi Crevice tool on the Panasonic Upright does the same job and it's a good deal cheaper. What do you think?"

I stared at The Hoover Man in stunned silence.

"They say the sound level on the K1 Pet Merlin is 63 decibels but, as I'm sure you know, they'll do anything to sell a new model. It's a load of bollocks. It's twice that level. Scared the shit out of my cat the first time I used it. The beast has never recovered. She's gone right off Hoovers." My heart went out to the poor feline, waiting every evening for the arrival of this lunatic. I could imagine it sitting there, nearing starvation, having to listen to the properties of the Merlin MCE3000 before there was any danger of exploring the comfort of Whiskas.

I was getting this treatment now for four hours each morning and it was beginning to disorient me. I was waking up during the night dreaming about

Hoovers - hostile Hoovers attacking me, their nozzles spitting fire. And so it went on into week three.

"What a day I had yesterday. I changed three deluxe Parquet heads and stripped a K3 Premium to the bare bones."

Day after day, the stories gushed forth. Every nut, bolt, and screw that had been turned, each nozzle that had been changed, every spare part that was not available, each Hoover bag that was the wrong size. I tried to change the subject, making suggestions that I thought might wean the Hoover Man's conversation off the subject of cleaning carpets. This was a forlorn hope. Even the most unlikely of topics found its way immediately to Hoovers.

"Interested in politics?" I ventured. Surely the maniac couldn't find a connection between politics and vacuum cleaners.

"Politics? Don't mention politics to me. A bunch of crooks, each and every one of them. There is only been one politician I've ever had any time for."

For a fleeting second I thought that I'd worked the miracle and got the Hoover Man onto another subject. I didn't give a fuck who the politician was – it could have been Hitler, as long as it didn't involve a Hoover. But of course it did.

"Herbert Clark Hoover. The greatest president the USA ever had. Son of a blacksmith, head of state from 1928 to1933. A man of extremely humble origins, he rose to be leader of the most powerful nation in the world. And I would appreciate it if you did not confuse him with J Edgar Hoover, an entirely different character, albeit also remarkable, having been head of the F.B.I. for nigh on fifty years."

For a second I thought that I was the subject of an elaborate scam, but one look at the Hoover Man convinced me otherwise.

"I like the name Hoover," he continued. "It's got a certain ring to it which vacuum cleaner lacks."

Suddenly he stopped and barked abruptly.

"Are you listening to me?"

By now I had lapsed into a state of semi-consciousness, but suddenly found myself nodding and then apologising for not giving the Hoover Man my full attention.

"As I was saying," the latter droned on, eyeing me suspiciously, "there's something not right with 'vacuum cleaner.' For instance, a vacuum is any

135

space in which there is no matter. So how do you clean an area where there's nothing? It doesn't make any sense. Anyway a perfect vacuum can never be attained. The closest you can get to it is interstellar space, and even I wouldn't go there for a job."

"Christ, what a pity," I thought, "It's the perfect place for you."

The weeks passed with the same routine being followed. The Hoover Man would arrive at around 10am and inundate me with tales of Hoovers for four hours, before setting off on another day's repair work. My attempts to change the subject were becoming feebler by the day, but, for some reason, I persevered. On another day I found myself pursuing the inevitable dead-end:

"Been abroad?" I attempted limply.

"Yeh, I spent a few years in the army. South America."

"What did you do in the army?"

"Bomb disposal."

This was sounding distinctly more hopeful.

"What was your favourite country in South America?"

"I don't know. They were all shit. Do you know I've been to places in Belize where they've never even seen a Hoover, let alone repaired one? Can you believe that! I was just thinking about it the other day with my head inside an Electrolux Vitesse Z407. Imagine never having seen one of these beauties! Hard to believe. Ever had one yourself? Especially good for dog hairs.'

In despair, I turned to football.

"Support a team, do you?"

"When I was younger I used to support a team called Cambuslang Rangers.   You'll not know them, they were a junior side, sponsored by Hoover as a matter of fact. They had a big factory next to the ground. I used to work there, made the original models. Beauties.   I've got twenty of them in my bedroom."

I finally broke at this remark. Something had to give. I stared at the Hoover Man.

"Twenty in your bedroom, eh? Have you one you could lend me?"

"And what would you be wanting with one of my Hoovers?" The Hoover Man looked at me suspiciously.

"Well I was wondering if they did services. I'm on my own at present and miss a bit of female company. I presume the Hoovers are female. I bet they could give you a good blow job."

We stared at each other across the bar, our eyes locked like two heavyweights awaiting the next punch. There was a long eerie silence. Eventually the Hoover Man took a drink of beer and very quietly said:

"Listen, you piece of shit, the only way you'll get near one of my Hoovers is over my dead body, but, be assured, I'll kill you before you're within a mile of them."

At this, he tossed the remainder of his pint into my face and made for the door, pausing briefly to throw me a menacing glance.

....

I brought in a book the following morning. There was a glorious silence in the bar, broken only by a distant hum as the cleaner, Ruby, worked on the carpet in the lounge. Two weeks passed. It was truly idyllic. Even when Ruby became ill and I had to take over cleaning duties, my mood remained optimistic, and the cleaning helped the dreary morning shift pass quickly. With the first signs of spring in the air, and the Hoover Man already becoming no more than a witty story, I arrived at work one morning to find a large, heavily wrapped package standing in the hallway. It was addressed to me, and in a state of high expectation, I hurriedly ripped the padding off. I could hardly believe my eyes. There before me stood a brand new, top of the range, gleaming vacuum cleaner. In a state of complete bemusement, I quickly opened the envelope that accompanied the strange cargo. The note inside the package contained a curious message:

"I'm going back to South America to teach the natives about the beauty of the Hoover. Here's a gift to show there's no hard feelings. It's the latest Dyson. A real humdinger. Takes you places you never dreamed about." The note was signed 'The Hoover Man.' It was only then that I realised I had never learned his name. Still, this really was a beautiful piece of equipment, a real classy machine. It would make cleaning the bar a pleasure. I hurried through to the lounge with his present and plugged it in. Perhaps I'd had been a bit harsh on the Hoover

Man. The phone rang at the bar as I was about to press the start button. I gave the Dyson to Ruby, who had returned to work that morning and was following events with great interest.

"Go ahead Ruby," I said, rushing through to the adjoining room to catch the call.

The explosion that wrecked the entire lounge knocked me from one end of the bar to the other. I struggled to my feet, bleeding profusely but still alive. The same, however, could not be said for Ruby, whose body parts were decorating what was left of the lounge. The Hoover Man had missed his target, but the pub was going to need a few builders and a new cleaner. Life had taken an unwelcome twist. Some head banger was trying to kill me. The world was truly full of nutters.

MARY IN THE MADHOUSE

After my adventures with Timmy and the Hoover Man my behaviour became rather odd. I was drinking like a fish, smoking cannabis by the sackful, snorting coke and swallowing anti-depressants. I'm not sure if the pills were working, as I was too out of my head to make an accurate appraisal. I was, however, sure that the Hoover Man's action had unnerved me. Okay, I'd been a bit sarcastic but he had surely reacted rather dramatically. I could have been injured. Poor old Ruby had been killed. And that fucker was still on the loose! What a lawless society. The authorities decided that another period in a mental hospital would be to my benefit. I was not against the idea as I needed a break from all the violence, a chance to reflect amongst some abundant greenery, and an escape from mainstream society. And there were more happy pills, which were fed to me by the fistful. It was also an opportunity to make new friends.

George was my first chum. A pleasant, plump young chap, George's life was never boring. He heard voices nearly all of the time and was therefore rarely alone. The voices had two sources; God and his brother-in law. George's brother-in-law lived in the trees surrounding the hospital and carried a sub-machine gun whose contents were destined for George the moment he stepped through the hospital gates. God gave George updates on the brother-in-law's exact location at any given moment, so that he knew exactly what tree the madman was hiding in. He used to point to this tree or that shouting wildly and asking me if I could see the nasty relation, but, although I tried my hardest, I never did catch a sight of the potential murderer. My favourite moments with George were break times when we would buy each other a cup of coffee. The problem was that we always ended up with four. George would buy one for himself and one for me and I would reciprocate. Then we would sit and wonder why we had four cups between the two of us. Fortunately, Charles, a country chap of some pedigree, would arrive and relieve us of a coffee for a shilling. Charles was single-handedly resisting decimalisation. This still left us with a spare coffee which would be taken by

142

Paul, who could have been a serf on Charles's estate in another time. There was a ritual to Paul's arrival. Firstly, he would doff his cap to Charles, who he referred to as "your lordship," and then he would ask who the spare coffee belonged to. I would reply "It's Peter Brady's, the invisible man." George would shake hands with the space occupied by the invisible man before sitting on top of him and drinking his coffee.

The staff, of course, kept a close eye on our jolly little company. We had all been slightly naughty in the past. I had helped poison a schoolmate, murdered two of my bosses, roasted my wife's cat and had been responsible for a pub being blown up and Ruby's three children becoming motherless. George had drowned his girlfriend who had also been hearing voices. What a pair! Apparently there had been a serious communication breakdown between the voices which accounted for the presence of the woman's brother in the trees. He was a bit miffed about George having killed his sister, but I had to sympathise with the tree man. My new friend, however, refused to accept that he had a case.

And there was Mary, who had knocked off her nasty husband. Mary Sparrow was my favourite companion in the happy farm. A quiet, self-effacing woman in her early fifties, she would sit of an afternoon and tell me the story of how she had committed the murder, acting out each character as though she was a one woman theatrical company. She had been married to John Sparrow, a highly successful businessman who had netted himself a considerable fortune playing with numbers on the stock exchange. He had a palatial home that blended well with the racehorses, the Ferrari and the Rolls. He also had Mary, who adored him. She was a loving, attentive mother who was making a fine job of raising his two beautiful daughters. She had kept his house in an immaculate condition, supervising the domestic staff in a thoroughly professional manner and attending to every domestic detail with unfailing efficiency.

Mary's outstanding quality, however, was her cooking skills. Sparrow had dined in five star restaurants all over Europe, but had never tasted food that came anywhere near the exquisite quality of his wife's cooking. The fact that she was French-trained obviously helped, but there was something extra that she brought to the art of cuisine, something personal and wonderful that distinguished her dishes from the rest. Every meal was unique, whether it was traditional Sunday roast or some exotic creation from the other side of the world. Mary also had another quality that suited Sparrow perfectly. She never asked questions as to his whereabouts. When he informed her that his business interests meant that he would be away from home every week from Friday morning to Sunday afternoon, she accepted this arrangement without question.

The Sparrows had not had carnal relations since the birth of their second daughter. Sex had stopped with the birth of Rachel, and had never returned. The couple had never confronted the situation and life continued as before, with the notable exception of physical intimacy. Sparrow, however, was a man used to overcoming problems and quickly decided that someone of his importance and financial clout could hardly be expected to go through life in a state of celibacy. He found the solution in the form of shapely Estelle, who was physically everything that Mary was not.

Estelle exuded sexuality, flaunting her femininity without any consideration of modesty. She wore dresses that highlighted every curve in her voluptuous body, leaving little to the imagination. She was flirtatious, passionate and, from the moment Sparrow kissed her crimson lips, he decided that she must become part of his empire. And Sparrow inevitably got what Sparrow wanted. Within a month he had established Estelle in a luxury West End apartment not far from his offices, but miles away from his mansion. She became the recipient of a monthly income that she could only have dreamed of in her previous life as a secretary. He also showered gifts upon her constantly. High maintenance indeed, but worth every penny.

Estelle, of course, was his weekend 'business trips.' Instead of listening to Mary garbling on about the servants or watching her read those infernal sexless books, Friday heralded the start of two days of unbridled sexual action, with Estelle catering to his every desire, which were many and varied.

146

Estelle knew what he needed, and went along with everything that was asked of her. She couldn't cook like Mary, of course. She couldn't cook at all in fact, but when welcomed by the naked Estelle of a Friday, the last thought on Sparrow's mind was food. There would be ample time for that on Sunday. The weekend contained a different 'dish of the day,' one you could really get your teeth into. It could not have panned out better for Sparrow. *Haute Cuisine* all week and hot sex all weekend. The arrangement was just perfect. He would return with his carnal needs satiated on a Sunday afternoon, to be cosseted and wonderfully fed by his unquestioning wife

.

Imagine then Sparrow's shock and dismay when, one rainy Friday night in mid December, he knocked at his mistress's door to find she was either out or, unbelievably, not answering. Sparrow didn't have a key. He'd never been let down in all the years of the arrangement and was confident enough to believe he didn't need one. He stood in the increasingly heavy rain for over thirty minutes, his temper becoming increasingly frayed as the downpour seeped through his suit. Something would have to be done about this. Sparrow was not a man to be messed around with. As he walked towards his car, he was already contemplating appropriate punishments for his wayward lover. He phoned Mary, mumbling about weather conditions and cancelled flights. "That's all right, John, just you come home. I'm preparing something special which we'll have when you get back."

Good old reliable Mary. She'd never let you down. Didn't have the imagination for a start. It had always amazed him that someone as intrinsically boring as his wife could be so creative in the kitchen. Strange, conjuring up all these exotic dishes then spending the rest of the evening in that awful grey cardigan reading books about plumbing, gardening, or the like. Always practical books about how to repair things, never as much as a novel. God she was dull. If only she had a bit more life about her, how different things could have been. Still, as long as she cooked like an angel and looked after the children, who cared what she read. It could have been the Koran for all the difference it made. He was missing Estelle's body already.

148

When he opened the front door, however, he was assailed by the most beautiful aroma imaginable, which temporarily took his mind off sex. "What a beautiful smell dear, what's on the menu tonight?" Sparrow asked confidently, knowing that even though this would be their first Friday night together in over two years, his wife would not discuss the reasons for his sudden arrival.

"Now you know I never give away the secrets of my kitchen, John, although, as this one is rather special, I might tell you about it after we've eaten." The pedestrian chat continued as the meal was served. It was simply the best that he'd ever tasted, even by his wife's ultra high standards. A rich succulent stew that melted in his mouth, complimented by a delicious sauce, which sent him into raptures.

"This really is the best you've ever made, dear What did you use?" Sparrow was genuinely interested.

"Oh, just a few new ingredients to create that special effect."

He asked for more and began wolfing into a second plateful when Mary said casually as if referring to an old friend.

"I met Estelle today. Very pretty." Sparrow put down his knife and fork and stared warily across the table. There was a prolonged silence before he cleared his throat and said slowly.

"How did you find out about Estelle?"

"I've known about Estelle for some time now. You were careless, John. You left a bill for her apartment in one of your pockets. That's when I had you followed. Very unlike you; you're usually so efficient. Anyway eat up, your dinner's getting cold. I wouldn't want anything to spoil your last meal."

Sparrow looked at what remained on his plate with a sense of growing unease.

"How's your stomach, John? According to my book, you should be experiencing   initial cramp pains by now."

Sparrow stared at his wife, with a look of disbelief.

"Is this some kind of joke?" he almost whispered.

But even as he spoke he felt a piercing pain streak across his abdomen.

"Now how could you imagine this being a joke, John? You know that I've no sense of humour, unlike your lovely Estelle who seemed positively chirpy before I cut her throat. I'll wager that the two of you had a good laugh about me when you

150

stopped for breath. Anyway I had to wipe the smile off her face before inviting her to join us for your last supper. It's nice that the three of us could be together for it, don't you think?"

"What have I been eating?"

Sparrow stared at his plate, a look of complete terror on his face, the searing pain in his stomach now continuous.

"Well I don't suppose you noticed, but since I found out about Estelle, I've been reading books on anatomy. It's remarkably easy to remove the heart and liver from a corpse given accurate instructions. We've just eaten those parts of the beautiful Estelle. I thought she was rather tasty, although naturally I didn't have the extra ingredients. They were just for my darling husband, whose fidelity I took for granted for such a long time. I've named the dish *Coeur D'Estelle* in honour of your lover. Anyway, I'm so glad you enjoyed her. In fact you can tell her yourself, you should have about ten minutes of agonising pain left before you die. I'll go and get her; she's in the other room."

As Sparrow held his stomach and gasped for air, Mary went through to the bedroom, returning with a wheelchair upon which was propped the remains of Estelle. Thick black blood matted her once blond hair. The anaesthetic had obviously been delivered by a hammer. Her throat had been cut and two gaping holes gaped from the places that once accommodated her heart and liver. Dried blood covered most of her distorted, mutilated body. Only her breasts were partially visible in the nightmare of mangled flesh that confronted the gasping Sparrow. But it was the face that transfixed him as he writhed in agony from the effects of the poison. Two blood filled empty sockets confronted him, where once had been Estelle's beautiful eyes. He groaned and vomited as the pain in his stomach worsened and death approached.

"What a shame. I've made a lovely dessert from Estelle's eyes, but I don't think you'll be quite up for it, darling. Concentrate on her breasts, I presume you liked fondling them and I can hardly blame you. I had a sneaky feel myself that   she let out a little groan as I touched them , but, to be totally honest, I think that was due to the effects of the hammer, rather than my touch. But what am I thinking of, my darling , is that   you're probably itching for a last intimate moment with what's left of her, before you depart. And why not? Let me bring your beautiful lover a bit closer to you."

She wheeled the remains of Estelle around to where John sat. His head was bowed and his face, caked with vomit, was convulsed in agony. "Now, a last touch of those once so beautiful breasts." She lifted Sparrow's limp hand to what was left of Estelle's breasts and, cupping his hand round the first, made him squeeze. He managed a weak scream as he felt the dried blood touch his fingers. "Now the other one dear, it still has the nipple intact, you'll like that. And I think a last kiss before you go. It might not be too pleasant as I removed Estelle's teeth before she died, just to keep as a memento" Mary, displaying remarkable power for such a frail woman, then forced the two heads together, one lifeless, the other screaming and vomiting. "There, that was sweet. Aye fond kiss." She replaced Sparrow to his original position and wheeled the bloody remains of Estelle back around the table. Lumps of his of vomit dropped slowly from her face onto the remains of her body. At this Sparrow gave up the fight for life and his head crashed into what remained of the Estelle stew on his plate.

"Goodness, John, you were so mistaken thinking that I'd lost my sense of romance. Who else could have arranged for you to die with your head on your lover's heart?

I had taken great liking to Mary and had her repeat the story many times. It impressed me deeply, especially her attention to detail. I had to turn down her offers of a cooked meal, of course. There was something about Mary. It had been good meeting a fellow murderer but I decided to stick to Mars Bars.

THE FAVOUR

I was eventually deemed sane enough to be released from the madhouse again, but as events unfolded this proved to be a poor decision. Initially I lived quietly, taking my pills, having my injections, visiting my social worker, and generally being a good citizen. But I'd surfaced again as a lonely nutter on the wrong side of the moon. I met Jackie who was also far from the Sea of Tranquillity. Jackie was a very beautiful woman, with high cheek bones and deep hazel-brown eyes. She would sit alone in the pub I frequented, sipping nothing but orange juice and speaking to no-one. I decided to introduce myself, buying her a drink, and attempting to sound normal. Unlike my encounter with the Hoover Man, all seemed well at the outset.

Jackie, however, was not only beautiful but extremely strange. She was good company when communicating, but sometimes our social life would become difficult as she chose to remain silent for long periods, staring straight in front of her in a most disconcerting manner. She'd moved to another moon. She rarely criticized others, which I thought extremely generous of her as the pub was full of wankers, most of whom would have been better dead in my opinion. But Jackie was loving and forgiving, and, as I planned horrible fates for Justin or Roger, she would excuse their boorish behaviour on childhood experiences at boarding school, or broken homes and the like. It was only when she discussed her ex-husband, Lawrence, that Jackie's mood changed. She became more than vengeful, she became homicidal. It was apparent that she had stored every negative feeling in life and found a place for them all in her virulent hatred of Lawrence.

The object of this animosity had sole custody of the one child of their marriage, a daughter of twelve. Lawrence had been not only granted complete control of Marie, but to add to Jackie's distress, she had not been allowed any access to her daughter. She had not seen her for over five years. To complete her misery, Jackie was not allowed to visit the picturesque little village where Lawrence, a lawyer of some standing, took care of the child. Try as I might, I could never prise from Jackie the circumstances leading up to this rather odd conclusion to a divorce. She would just growl that 'shitface', as she consistently referred to her ex, had won everything because he was a lawyer and knew the right people. This explanation did not ring totally true but, though I tried to get to the bottom of the story, my partner always clammed up when the questions became intimate.

After a few months the subject of shitface and Marie temporarily fell off the radar and weeks went by without it being mentioned. I was becoming accustomed to a peaceful life when the 'favour' reared its head.

"There's something I want you to do for me," she said one night, sipping at her orange juice, "but you'll refuse."

"Well it would help if I knew what you wanted, then I'll be able to say yes or no. D'you need a lift somewhere?"

I'd managed to get my hands on an old jalopy and felt rather useful for once.

"It's not a lift," she replied, a note of agitation in her voice, "it's more important than that…anyway, you'll not do it."

The conversation dragged on in this vein for almost an hour before we agreed that she'd tell me the favour the following night over a curry.

We met the next evening, same time, same place. There was one difference, however. Jackie was drinking large vodkas with her fresh orange juice. By the time we reached the restaurant she was swaying slightly and slurring her words. Ignoring the menu, she ordered two bottles of red wine as we took our seats. She slugged the first glass as though there was a crisis in the European vineyards, poured another, and stared at me.

"Right, what the fuck is the favour, Jackie?"

I was becoming rather irritated by this game. The favour was annoying me.

"My auntie died last month and she left me ten thousand pounds." Another long stare.

"Good. What you going to do with it? Buy a vineyard?"

Straight faced, the owl eyes were on me.

"No, I'm going to give it to you if you do me the favour."

"It must be a big favour. What is it? Will you buy me a Mars Bar too?"

I'd told Jackie my shoplifting story, which had produced a rare smile. Humour wasn't high on her agenda.

"Let's get back to your place and I'll tell you." We wobbled back through the cobbled streets, stopping briefly for a bottle of Blue Label, in case either of us could still speak. I was by now thoroughly convinced that Jackie was mad, and that I'd never find out what the fucking favour was.

Stare, stare. Glug, glug. Puff, puff.

"Okay. What the bloody hell to you want me to do that's worth ten thousand quid."

She responded immediately. "I want you to kill my ex-husband." No emotion, the same owl stare. "I need to see my daughter again."

Two weeks later I was shown into the lawyer's office in the quiet little border town. If I was going to kill this fucker I wanted to have a look at him first. Red shirt with white collar, wispy little beard, no moustache and balding. His appearance sealed his fate. He deserved extermination, merely for looking like that. He had declared war on taste. I asked politely about the shirt but he basically told me to mind my own business. I talked to him briefly about the fictitious reason for my visit, which he immediately dismissed, asking me to leave his pristine little office immediately as he felt I was not being serious, and my complaint was ridiculous. I suggested that his shirt was more ridiculous before exiting. Smug little bastard. And he was so much older than Jackie, dirty old wrinkled piece of shit. It was going to be a pleasure whacking this ratbag. His outrageous behaviour with my girlfriend apart, he had been extremely rude to me when I asked about suing the World Wildlife Fund after it had refused to support my perfectly rational request to keep a group of penguins in my communal back garden. The pompous little rat described my proposal as crazy. Several large hotels nearby had peacocks. Peacocks....penguins....they're all the same. Just bloody birds. I was going to show the fucker what 'crazy' meant.

I booked a room in a hotel directly opposite his office. From there I could watch his comings and goings. It was also near his sea view villa allowing me to spend a week observing the target, his wife, and Jackie's daughter. He'd certainly gone for the more mature type. The spouse was straight out of

'Horse and Hound.' The lawyer had traded sexiness for sturdiness. This was a nightmare in tweed and facial hair. The daughter was less visually offensive, if a tad on the plain side. She was,however, completely overshadowed by the large hairy woman alongside her.

.

It was Larry the lawyer who was to command my attention, however. I watched his movements for four days. He left the office each night at seven on the dot and walked home. This made things much easier. I was waiting for him on the second Friday evening of my stay outside his vast driveway. The act itself was simple. Just a whack on the forehead with the hammer, followed by the transference of the corpse to my car. Unfortunately, the corpse started making gurgling noises as I opened the boot on reaching the part of the cliff that was to be its final resting point. As I started to drag the bloodied lump of flesh to the drop, it stared at me and gasped:
"Why?"
"Because of the way you treated Jackie."
"But I had to get rid of her; she was stealing all our money."

"You could have let her see her child" I replied, for once in my life adopting the moral high ground, as I pulled him by his legs towards the edge of the cliff.

"She was our child minder" he groaned.

I felt rather confused as I watched the body hurtling through the air towards the ocean

....

I met Jackie the following day in a café back in town and asked her about the money. I was tense, wanting to get the transaction completely concluded with minimal fuss. She looked at me.

"Is he dead?" Her face was white, her expression blank.

"He's in the sea."

She went into her bag and produced a large brown envelope which she threw onto the table in front of me. On top of it she carefully placed a Mars Bar.

"There." She smiled sweetly. "Now you've got something more important to feel guilty about."

"So have you, mummy. He talked to me before he died."

"And you believed him?"

"Hard to say," I replied, pocketing the cash and taking a bite of the Mars Bar, before walking out the door.

BODY PARTS IN BANGKOK

My brain has turned against me now because I've grown old. Its ageist and nasty with it. As my twilight years approach, the convoluted nervous tissue in my skull has started going on journeys by itself, leaving me to deal with my creaking body on my own. I've began to take bus journeys to distant places while by brain takes the correct bus home. By the time I arrive at back at my flat, flustered and needing pills, I find my brain sitting on the settee finishing off a Marks and Spencer's meal for two washed down with a bottle of Pinot Noir. I order it back into my head, and, although it eventually complies, I can hear it chortling from inside me in a most disconcerting manner. Sometimes I'll pop into the kitchen and suddenly wonder why I'm there. Returning to the lounge, I'll find my exasperating organ sitting on the sofa, smiling at me in the way only my brain can, whilst apparently enjoying 'Loose Women' on the television, a programme it knows that I, a man of refined taste, find particularly repellent. That's only one of its games.

With women, my brain's behaviour leads to unbelievably embarrassing situations. It conspires with my pancreas, a particularly gullible organ, to limit the amount of blood to my penis in moments of intimacy. My doctor has described this as a side effect of age and diabetes, but he knows nothing about it; he's not heard my brain laughing, when, at the moment of penetration, instead of being in charge of nine inches of throbbing flesh, I find myself staring at a sad chipolata on the day after Christmas. I prefer chess to women anyway, regardless of how loose they are, but my brain has made my pursuit of the game practically impossible these days. When I spot a particularly powerful move, say a gambit or a fianchetto, my cantankerous body part compels me to place my queen directly on the opposition's diagonal, to be gobbled up by a surprised if grateful bishop.

My brain also relishes in hurting me physically. It encourages me to pick up saucepans which are obviously too hot to handle, and sniggers maliciously as I run my raw fingers under the cold tap. It positively insists that when the season changes and snow covers the ground I wear shoes that leak, and forget my keys. Sometimes it varies the latter and convinces me to leave the keys in the lock as I depart, enabling burglars to enter the house with the least possible fuss. And, of course, there is the traffic. There are few things that provide it with greater pleasure that forcing me to stagger across busy streets forcing cars and buses to swerve to avoid the suicidal idiot bouncing around the centre of a rush-hour six-lane highway, playing dodge the traffic. Its remarkable how many motorists prefer crashing into each other, rather than knock a pedestrian down. It has restored my faith in my fellow man. Not in that sod in my skull, however. Any faith in a treaty with that thing has been well and truly dashed by its latest shenanigans.

Recently, the lump of grey matter has gone a step further in its attempt to ruin my wellbeing. It has started to collude with my other organs to ensure that my later years are most uncomfortable and has combined with my liver to produce a sinister partnership. For decades my liver was more than happy dealing with my waste products, cleaning my system and handling the excesses of booze and drugs which I piled upon it with gay abandon. Now it's threatening all out strike action. A small amount of alcohol these days makes me feel extremely ill and I turn a peculiar yellowish green colour. It has also been in contact with my lungs which have started objecting to even the occasional cigarette.

These most inconvenient actions of my nefarious organ I have learned to live with, but things reached a disastrously new low a few weeks ago when my brain stole my soul. There I was one day happily talking to my soul about the intrinsic goodness of mankind when suddenly everything went blank and I passed into a coma. Waking up, I realised that my soul had disappeared. I searched high and low, needing to have a chat about the time when our distant ancestors lived in a cooperative, selfless, loving, innocent state, but my soul was nowhere to be found. My brain had taken it to a dark distant place, where no man has ever gone.

That's why I'm lying in a hotel room in Phatchahung Alley, Bangkok, overlooking the Soi Cowboy bar where they have pussy ping pong and the wretched of the earth sell their bodies to the scum of the earth. Lady boy meets cowboy. The insurance salesman from Oregon finally meets a sexy woman and she's got balls as an added extra. I watch them from my window, surrounded by fifty packets of Marlboro, (I've had a strict word with my lungs on this issue), five litres of Jack Daniels, a large rock of cocaine, and the delightful Wan Li. This has hurt me financially but, what the hell, Jackie's ten grand has allowed me to slip the brain, which is still in Edinburgh airport wondering where I am. It'll find me eventually and exact a final brutal revenge, but in the meantime I have plenty to occupy me here, and to my surprise there are loads of places selling Mars Bars.

So I spend the days with Wan Li, shagging, falling over, and thinking about the arrival of the world's end, which is fast approaching. The coming of the Antichrist has certainly added an interest to my life. The blood red moons are in the sky and we're all going together on judgement day. And the Antichrist doesn't fuck around. No prisoners, no letters from your mother. The world is about to enter a catastrophic spiral as predicted in the Good Book. I thought I'd be going to eternal damnation on my own after Tom Dow, Braithwaite, Jimmy the painter, Larry the lawyer, and the cat, but by all reliable reports we're going together, which is a bit of a relief. The Israelis kick things off by dropping a few nuclear bombs on The Palestinians after one of their soldiers gets his finger cut in a rocket attack and it escalates from there. Iran manages to graze a settler's knee and, Bob's your uncle, Armageddon.

I try to explain this to Wan Li and the cat, Vesuvius, but as neither speaks English, it's a thankless task. Vesuvius seems to respond to the first syllable of *cata*strophic, but that could be my imagination, and when Wan Li meets the Antichrist she'll negotiate a rate for a blow job. She's at the moment sitting across from me snorting coke and guzzling Mars Bars. I'll have to reduce her in intake of the latter as she is putting on weight by the day. She's turning into an Asian Janet Ralston.

So that's about that. The red moon is in full above me, debauchery fills the streets below. I eat another Mars bar, as the creatures in the bars play ping-pong pussy. Thankfully, it will all be over soon.

Ken Bridges was in born in Glasgow, sometime in the last century. After being educated at Edinburgh University, he worked in a series of ridiculous jobs, culminating in teaching. He has had a number of short stories published. This is his first novel.

Made in the USA
Charleston, SC
31 July 2016